PACKING IRON

Rebellious teenager Raven Bjorkman and her widowed mother, Ingrid, save the life of Gabriel Moonlight, an outlaw dying from gunshot wounds. They learn that he was shot by his enemy's son, Stadtlander, a ruthless rancher. Gabriel rides off, leaving Raven and Ingrid caring deeply for him. Then, when they move to Old Calico in California, they are unexpectedly reunited with Gabriel who finds himself in a perilous situation where only his gun-skills will save the day.

STEVE HAYES

PACKING IRON

Complete and Unabridged

LINFORD
Leicester

First published in Great Britain in 2009 by
Robert Hale Limited
London

First Linford Edition
published 2011
by arrangement with
Robert Hale Limited
London

British Library CIP Data

Hayes, Steve.
  Packing iron. - - (Linford western library)
  1. Western stories.
  2. Large type books.
  I. Title II. Series
  823.9'2–dc22

ISBN 978–1–4448–0733–2

Published by
F. A. Thorpe (Publishing)
Anstey, Leicestershire

Set by Words & Graphics Ltd.
Anstey, Leicestershire
Printed and bound in Great Britain by
T. J. International Ltd., Padstow, Cornwall

This book is printed on acid-free paper

For you, Cora

Prologue

From her hiding place among the rocks Raven watched the lone horse limping across the hot, sun-baked desert toward her. The all-black stallion, a once-magnificent-looking Morgan, was sweat-caked and exhausted and blood from its wounded rider glistened on its flanks.

The horse moved slowly, each wobbly step a painful effort. Too weak to keep its head up, parched tongue lolling from its foam-slathered mouth, the animal was on its last legs.

Raven wondered what kept the stallion going. Other than the well by her folks' cabin there was no water within miles and in this intense New Mexico heat she knew the horse must be dangerously dehydrated.

As for the hatless man slumped motionless over the saddle, a tall, big-shouldered man with long tangled dark hair hanging over his face, she guessed he was already dead. And if he wasn't, she knew he soon would be. The buzzards circling ominously in the cloudless, eye-achingly blue sky overhead would soon make sure of that.

A slim, grubby-looking girl, almost fourteen, whose short crow-black hair, big black eyes and sun-faded denim shirt and jeans gave her a tomboy look, Raven watched impatiently as the horse drew level with her. How long would she have to wait, she wondered, before the horse collapsed and she could collect the dead man's weapons — a well-used holstered Peacemaker with ebony grips, a bone-handled hunting knife and an old Model 73 Winchester tucked into a scabbard.

As if answering her question the man suddenly slipped from the saddle and collapsed on the burning sand. The foot nearest her was still hooked in the stirrup and the Morgan, feeling the man's weight dragging, stopped, legs trembling, flanks heaving.

Scrambling down from the rocks Raven cautiously approached the horse, waiting to see how it would react. Fighting off its exhaustion, the stallion bared its teeth at her. Not wanting to get bitten or kicked, Raven hunkered down a few yards away and made soothing sounds in hopes of gaining its trust.

Within moments she had company. All around her the buzzards landed in a wing-flapping rush, screeching and pecking at each other for position. Enraged, the horse wheeled and charged them, scattering the big ugly birds from its path. The sudden movement caused the man's boot to jerk free of the stirrup, leaving him sprawled on his side in the dirt. Raven now saw that his jeans and shirt were soaked with blood and realized he'd been shot in the lower back.

She moved close to him — only to have to jump aside as the exhausted stallion wheeled again and wearily charged her. Raven easily avoided it.

The Morgan turned, pausing to gather its strength, only to see the buzzards closing in on their prey. The horse charged again, squealing with rage as it tried to bite them. The birds scattered. But persistent as death, they quickly returned and once more hopped close to the man.

Again, the stallion charged and again the buzzards scattered and then returned for their meal. With each charge the horse grew weaker. Finally, it stopped charging and stood protectively by the man, flanks heaving, too exhausted to move.

The buzzards formed a circle around man and horse, and patiently began their death watch . . .

Admiring the horse's effort to protect its rider, Raven took a slingshot from her back pocket, loaded it with a stone, aimed low so as not to kill the bird and let go. The stone struck the buzzard in the body. It screeched and flew aloft. Alarmed, the other birds followed suit. Raven, knowing they would soon return, spoke soothingly to the stallion, all the time inching closer. The Morgan snorted, and glared at her with blazing red eyes but made no move to bite or kick her.

Kneeling beside the inert man, Raven kept her eye on the horse as she gently eased the big Colt .45 from its holster. It took a few moments. As she finally pulled the gun loose, the man's right hand suddenly grasped her wrist, startling her. Realizing he was still alive, she tried to jerk free but even near death he was too strong for her.

Through the dark, sweat-matted hair caked to his forehead she saw him staring at her. His eyes, deep-set and paler than any blue eyes she'd ever seen, seemed to pierce her like bullets. She tried to think of something to say, but before any words formed the man's eyes clouded over and he passed out.

Raven quickly pried his fingers open and, still holding the gun, jumped up and ran off. When she reached the rocks, she stopped and looked back at the man. *He hadn't moved. But the stallion now sank to its knees and flopped onto its side, the breath from its flared nostrils stirring the sand in little spurts.*

Immediately, the buzzards returned, circling their prey and once more beginning their grim death watch.

Holding the pistol with both hands, Raven aimed above the birds and fired. She'd never shot a handgun before and wasn't prepared for the recoil. Her hands kicked upward, sending the bullet wild of its mark. But the echoing boom frightened the buzzards, chasing them aloft where they began circling.

Satisfied, Raven took a final look at man and horse, decided the Winchester and hunting knife could wait, and ran off.

1

New Mexico

It was late afternoon. The desert sunlight flooding in through the open barn doors cast long shadows over the woman tending to a wounded man lying on a pile of straw.

The woman, a young widow named Ingrid Bjorkman, was pretty in a fair-skinned, wholesome way. Small and slim, she had large blue eyes, a wide mouth shaped for smiling and sun-streaked tawny hair that she kept tied in a bun behind her head. She looked too gentle for the harsh, arid environment she was living in; yet the very fact she was here, with calluses on her slender, elegant hands, recent scratches on her legs and dried bloodstains soiling her cotton print dress proved that she was no quitter.

Finished bathing the stranger's face, she gently placed the wet cloth across his forehead. Then uncorking a bottle of rye that she kept for medicinal purposes only, she poured a small amount into a cup and pressed it against his parched lips. It took a moment, but finally she managed to pry them open, allowing a little whiskey to trickle into his mouth. His eyelids fluttered but didn't open. The woman repeated the procedure, then corked the bottle, set it down and studied her patient.

He was taller and rangier than her late husband, Sven, who had inherited his Norwegian father's massive shoulders and barrel chest, but looked as if he had great stamina. She guessed his age to be anywhere between 35 and 45. But despite all her efforts to save his life — cutting out the bullet lodged in his lower back, cauterizing the wound with the white-hot blade of his knife and then bandaging it with torn strips of sheet — by then the stranger had lost so much blood she sensed he wouldn't live long enough to see his next birthday.

That would be a shame, she thought. Even unconscious, his rugged, chiseled face possessed the integrity of a mountain. And by the jut of his jaw, Ingrid sensed this man had grit and determination and knew she was looking at no ordinary drifter or desert rider.

Hearing a whinny outside, she hurried to the door. The all-black stallion that Raven had earlier hand-fed water until it struggled weakly to its feet was now fully recovered. It stood in the corral looking over the fence at the hot desert scrubland.

Ingrid followed its gaze and in the distance saw a plume of dust trailing the wagon racing toward her. Two slender girls sat in the wagon, one handling the reins; while riding alongside them were three Apache horsemen. Ingrid's heart pumped faster. She knew they would not be there if her daughter hadn't succeeded in her mission.

★ ★ ★

Earlier, when Raven had come running up to her outside their cabin, Ingrid had chided her for conveniently disappearing when it came time to hang out the wash. Nor did she believe her daughter's story about a man dying from a gunshot wound in the desert just over the rise.

'Lying only makes it worse,' Ingrid scolded. 'I've a good mind to send you to bed without your supper.'

'If I'm lying,' Raven said, producing the six-gun from under her shirt, 'then where'd I get this from?'

For a moment Ingrid was too surprised to speak. Then she quickly told Raven to hitch up the team while she got the iodine and bandages and filled a canteen with water.

'Hurry,' she cried as Raven ran to the barn. 'We must do all we can to save this man.'

2

As the wagon and horsemen drew closer to the cabin Ingrid recognized the two young Apaches as Walking Man and Runs With Head Up. Since settling in the desert fifteen years ago, she and Sven had often talked to them during their many visits to the nearby Mescalero reservation.

The third and much older man, Almighty Sky, she knew was the tribal shaman. A shape-shifter, supposedly capable of becoming any animal or bird he chose, he was famous for his uncanny ability to predict the future. It was he, in fact, who in 1886 had predicted that Geronimo would be captured.

A year later Sven's father, Johan, while out hunting had rescued Almighty Sky from marauding Comanches who had covered his naked body with wild honey and staked him over an anthill. From then on Johan, his family and their descendants never worried about being attacked by Apaches.

Almighty Sky rarely ventured from the reservation and on any other occasion Ingrid would have been impressed to see him. But today her eyes were riveted on the young Apache girl sitting on the wagon box beside Raven. Despite the intense heat she clasped a white blanket about her, revealing little of the beaded white doeskin dress underneath or her matching knee-high moccasins. No more than sixteen, her impassive, beautiful face was framed by long prematurely white hair, and her large almond-shaped eyes were completely covered by milky cataracts.

Ingrid had never seen her before. But like most white settlers in the area she'd heard of this remarkable girl whom the Apaches revered and considered sacred. Named Lolotea, which is Apache for Gift from God, she was a blood relative of the famous Mescalero warrior woman Dahteste, who was presently in custody with Geronimo and other renegade Apaches in a government-controlled village at Fort Sill, Oklahoma.

According to the Apaches, Lolotea possessed unearthly healing powers. In the short time she'd been alive legends had sprung up around her. 'Some say she even has the power of life and death,' Sven told Ingrid. 'Of course, that can't be true. But for there to be so many stories about her, there has to be some truth to her healing ability.'

Because of this gift, and the fact that Lolotea was totally blind, she was not permitted to leave the reservation and was guarded day and night by Walking Man and Runs With Head Up. But now, as a favor to Ingrid, here she was ready to try to heal the stranger Raven had found dying in the desert.

Shortly, the wagon and horsemen reined up in front of Ingrid. She smiled at Almighty Sky but did not thank him for allowing the 'Sacred One' to come

13

here as she knew he would consider it impolite. Instead, she stood with Raven and watched as the two braves helped Lolotea down and led her into the barn. Presently, both reappeared and stood guard so no one could enter and disturb her.

'We must leave the Sacred One alone now,' Almighty Sky told Ingrid. 'It is not for us to witness the miracle about to occur.'

'Perhaps you and your warriors would honor my home with your presence,' she replied in faltering Apache. 'I have tobacco and lemons for lemonade.'

'I am unworthy of such hospitality,' the old Medicine Man said. 'But if it pleases you I, alone, will accept.'

Inside, the one-bedroom cabin was spartanly furnished but comfortable. Four oak chairs and a table that had belonged to Ingrid's deceased parents occupied the center of the main room, while a china cupboard and a wood-burning stove purchased in nearby

Santa Rosa stood against the wall by the pantry. The bedroom was just big enough to hold two single beds and an armoire, while on the wall facing the window was an oil portrait of Sven and Ingrid on their wedding day.

Almighty Sky sat at the table and 'made smoke', using the tobacco and cigarette papers that had belonged to Sven and which Ingrid still kept in an old coffee can in the cupboard.

Raven helped her mother cut and squeeze the lemons and when the lemonade was ready, she brought the pitcher and three glasses to the table. She did not speak to the old Medicine Man, or even meet his gaze, for both would have been disrespectful; she was therefore surprised when he suddenly spoke to her.

He called her *Ish-kay-nay*, which in Apache means 'boy' or 'one who is indifferent to marriage' — or in Raven's case 'tomboy' — and despite his age and tribal importance respected her enough not to ask her a direct question.

'I have many sons and grandsons, *Ish-kay-nay*, but this old man would be proud to have a daughter such as you.'

'I am pleased to hear this,' Raven said politely, 'but I do not deserve such an honor.'

Almighty Sky exhaled a cloud of smoke and watched it spiral to the ceiling. Then he nodded solemnly, as if agreeing with her, and turned to Ingrid.

'*Nah-tanh*,' he said, which was Apache for cornflower and also the color of her eyes, 'it must bring you pleasure to have raised a child so courteous.'

'Great pleasure,' she said. She smiled at Raven, whose fiery, precocious personality and dark coloring were so different from her parents. 'I only regret that her father will miss the joy of seeing her grow into womanhood.'

'Death is a white man's word, *Nah-tanh*. Apaches believe that a loved one's spirit always remains with us and therefore sees and hears everything.'

'I have heard this,' Ingrid said. She

gazed sadly about her, thinking how comforting it would be if Sven's spirit was her constant companion. 'Perhaps when more time passes, I too will be able to feel my husband's presence.'

She paused as soft, melodic chanting came from the barn.

'The healing has begun,' Almighty Sky said. 'Now the pale eyes' life is in the hands of the Great Spirit.'

★   ★   ★

Outside in the corral the stallion also heard the chanting and pricked its ears forward. It whinnied quietly and pawed at the ground.

Walking Man and Runs With Head Up, still guarding the entrance to the barn, watched as the horse backed away from the corral fence, tossed its head and then reared up.

They weren't surprised. They knew it was the Spirit god talking to the stallion, assuring it that its master would not die.

3

Lolotea kept constant vigil over the wounded stranger. Every so often she chanted softly, her milky-white eyes gazing blindly into space, one hand placed upon his wound, the other on her heart. She used no medicine or ancient tribal remedy to cure him, knowing he was beyond earthly help. Instead, she prayed to *Yusan*, the Mescalero god of creation, begging him to relinquish his hold on the white man's spirit and allow him to remain in this world.

Night fell. Supper came and went. Raven grudgingly helped her mother wash and dry the dishes then stole some sugar and went outside to feed it to the stallion.

Ingrid, feeling helpless, offered to take food to Lolotea. But Almighty Sky wouldn't permit it. In her present holy state, he explained, the Sacred One could not eat, drink or speak to anyone. Bidding her goodnight, the old shaman left the cabin and bedded down by the wood pile. He fell asleep dreaming he was the leader of a pack of gray wolves hunting the moon. It was a strange dream but even stranger was the fact that high above him the dark clouds closing in on the moon were shaped like wolves.

Ingrid, who slept next to the bedroom window, awoke during the night and heard the stallion acting up in the corral.

It reminded her of the stranger fighting for his life in the barn. Unanswered questions raced through her mind. Who was he? Who had shot him? Did he have a wife or a family? Was he, as Raven had said, an outlaw? Was he on the run from a posse? If he were, it would explain why he'd been shot. And most importantly, she wondered, why did she have a strange feeling about him, a feeling that told her he would become a vital part of her and Raven's lives?

Somewhere off in the distance a coyote yip-yipped. It was a mournful, lonely sound and though it was an integral part of the desert and one familiar to Ingrid, she shivered. The face of the stranger suddenly appeared before her. It was so real she was startled. She blinked and the face disappeared, leaving her wondering if she'd had a vision. Disturbed, she lay there thinking about what was happening in the barn. The idea that his life depended upon the unique powers of a girl barely older than Raven was almost beyond comprehension and made Ingrid appreciate just how mystical life was among the Apaches.

Turning on her side, she looked at her daughter sleeping peacefully in the other bed. As always, Ingrid felt an overwhelming love for Raven. She had felt it from the instant she had cradled the newborn baby in her arms. 'I don't know what it is about her,' she told

Sven after the midwife had left, 'but I sense she is truly special.'

He agreed with her. 'She's what my great-grandfather called a 'Tenth Generation Child'.' He went on to explain how every ten generations a child was born into his family with Raven's coloring. They were known as 'Fiona babies.' Fiona, Sven added, was the name of a wild and beautiful, raven-haired heathen Irish princess whom his Norsemen ancestors had kidnapped almost a thousand years ago on one of their raids along the coast of Ireland. During the return voyage to Norway, rather than remain a prisoner she had stabbed herself with a dagger. But before dying she cursed her captors for abducting her and warned them that every hundred years she would return and make their lives a living hell.

Looking at Raven now, Ingrid smiled and thought how unlike Fiona's curse her daughter was. Not only was Raven a good child, a blessing in fact, but if it were not for her Ingrid would have no reason for living. At the same time, though, she had to admit that Raven was precocious, incredibly stubborn and often rebellious, so perhaps there was some truth in Fiona's curse.

Earlier, upon entering the bedroom, she had found Raven kneeled beside her bed, finishing her prayers. 'And please, dear God, keep the stranger alive. Amen.'

When Raven saw her mother watching her from the door, she said: 'Was I wrong to ask God that, Momma? I mean, we don't know anything about him. For all we know he may be a gunfighter or an outlaw. And then I've asked the Lord to save a bad man.'

'No matter who he is,' Ingrid said, tucking her into bed. 'It's never wrong to ask God to save a life.'

Raven looked relieved. 'What I can't figure out,' she said sleepily, 'is why I care if he lives or dies.'

Since rescuing the wounded stranger, Ingrid had asked herself the same question. 'Perhaps it's because he's a human being and if he dies then a tiny part of us dies along with him.'

Raven didn't believe that. People in Santa Rosa were always dying and she didn't feel any sense of loss for them.

'Maybe it's 'cause I found him, Momma. You know, like when you find a bird with a broken wing and you bring it home to look after — you always want it to live and feel so sad when it dies.'

'Perhaps,' Ingrid said. 'Now, go to sleep, child. You have chores tomorrow.'

★   ★   ★

At first light, before even the rooster crowed, Ingrid dressed and took a dipper of water to the barn. Walking Man and Runs With Head Up hadn't moved from their post, but Apache-fashion had taken catnaps while standing up.

Waiting until each brave took a grateful sip, Ingrid then asked Walking Man if he knew how the patient was.

23

'He is still with this world,' a voice said behind her.

Relieved, she turned and saw it was Almighty Sky. 'Is there anything I can do? Anything he needs?' she asked. 'I could heat up some broth. It would only take a minute.'

'Patience, *Nah-tanh*,' Almighty Sky gently chided her. 'Miracles cannot be rushed.'

4

It was late afternoon when Almighty Sky summoned Ingrid to the barn. Raven, who was helping her mother repair the fence around the vegetable garden, insisted on going with her.

'I found him, Momma. I got a right to be there.'

'It's not up to me, lamb. But if Almighty Sky doesn't mind, then you're welcome as far as I'm concerned.'

When they entered the barn they found Almighty Sky sitting cross-legged beside the stranger. Nearby, Walking Man and Runs With Head Up stood guarding Lolotea, who lay trance-like under her white blanket on some straw.

'You must not speak to her,' Almighty Sky told Ingrid and Raven. 'She is in her most sacred state.'

Ingrid knew he meant Lolotea and the Great Spirit had become one and nodded to show she understood. She then indicated the wounded man. His eyes were still closed and he showed no sign of life. 'I see no change in him,' she said, disappointed. 'Is he going to live?'

'It is written, *Nan-tanh*. The Sacred One has told me this. The stranger's spirit will not be taken from him.'

'Thank God.' Ingrid looked at Lolotea, who hadn't moved. 'How can I ever repay her?'

'The Sacred One needs no earthly reward, Nan-tanh. Her joy comes from serving the Great Spirit. That is reward enough.'

'What I'd like to know,' Raven said impatiently, 'is did the Great Spirit say when the stranger will wake up and start talking?'

'Hush! Where are your manners?' Ingrid scolded.

'It is all right,' Almighty Sky assured her. 'To be young is to be impulsive.' To Raven he said: 'You will see his eyes soon. Now, go with your mother and prepare broth. The stranger will be hungry when he returns among us.'

While her mother was heating up the broth Raven heard the stallion whinnying. She ran to the cabin door. The Morgan stood at the corral fence watching Walking Man and Runs With Head Up bridling their horses outside the barn.

'They're leaving, Momma!'

Surprised, Ingrid removed the broth from the flame and ran outside with her daughter.

'Please, take our wagon,' she begged Almighty Sky. 'I'll send Raven for it in a day or two.'

'There is no need, *Nan-tanh*. The Sacred One has chosen to ride.'

A slender, white-clad, ethereal figure appeared in the barn doorway. It was Lolotea, her long white hair now platted into braids. The sunlight framed her beautiful pale face, encircling it like a halo. Like a visiting angel, she looked back at the stranger. His eyes were now open and, though still weak, he was conscious of her mystical presence.

'*Sadnleel da ya'dee nzho*,' she told him softly. 'Long life, old age, and everything good.'

He nodded his thanks and watched as she walked to the horses. Walking Man had already spread her white blanket over his pony's back. Helping her to mount, he grasped the reins and led her away.

'God bless you,' Ingrid said softly as Lolotea rode past.

Lolotea looked at Ingrid with her milky, sightless eyes and smiled. It was a smile of unspoiled innocence and Ingrid felt warmed by it. She watched as the Apaches headed out into the burning desert. In her mind she heard Sven's voice saying: 'Some say Lolotea even has the power of life and death. Of course, that can't be true . . . '

Ingrid had believed him at the time. Now she wasn't so sure. After all, there was a stranger in the barn who by rights should be dead. Yet he wasn't and that was one miracle she couldn't explain.

5

Almighty Sky was right: the stranger, now awake, was indeed hungry. As he greedily sipped broth from the spoon held by Raven, who'd insisted on feeding him, Ingrid introduced herself and her daughter. When he didn't respond, she asked him his name.

Instead of answering her, he fixed his ice-blue eyes on Raven and said hoarsely: 'Y-You're the girl in the desert . . . one who tried to steal my gun.'

If he expected her to be repentant, he was mistaken.

'You would've done the same, mister, if you thought I was dead.'

'Raven — !'

'It's true, Momma. He would've. Anybody would've. Wouldn't you?' she demanded, holding the spoon just out of reach of his mouth. 'C'mon. Admit it.'

He said only: 'I'd rot in hell 'fore I'd rob a dead man.'

'An' hell's where you'd be if I hadn't found you.'

'Raven, how dare you!' Ingrid glared at her rebellious daughter. 'Apologize immediately.'

'Why? I ain't sorry I said it. I saved his life and now he's calling me a thief!' Raven angrily pushed the bowl and spoon into her mother's hands and ran out of the barn.

'Please, forgive her,' Ingrid said. 'Raven looks full grown but emotionally, my goodness she's still a child . . .'

He was too weak to care. Wearily closing his eyes, he continued sipping the broth.

When the bowl was empty Ingrid patted his lips dry with her apron and stood up. The stranger hadn't opened his eyes since he'd finished eating and she thought he was asleep. Quietly, so as not to awaken him, she started to leave.

'Brandy . . . ?' he whispered hoarsely.

'I'm afraid I don't have any. I do have whiskey — '

'No, no . . . my horse . . . Brandy . . . is he . . . ?'

'Oh, he's fine,' she assured him. 'He's out there in the corral. But any time you like, I can bring him into the barn.'

For an instant, relief flickered in the man's uncannily pale blue eyes. Then it was gone and he weakly shook his head.

'Leave him be . . . ' He closed his eyes and was asleep before Ingrid could say another word.

* * *

When he next awoke it was night. Raising himself up on his elbows, he looked around. A kerosene lamp glowed nearby. By its light he saw an old wagon parked against the rear wall, a well-worn bridle hanging from a hook, a pitchfork leaning against a stall and feed piled in one corner. So, he thought, nothing has changed. I am still here — wherever here is.

31

'Feeling better?' The same blue-eyed woman with the pleasing smile and butter-colored hair who'd fed him earlier now leaned into his vision. When he nodded she asked him if he was hungry. He nodded again. The woman disappeared and, when she returned a little later, she carried a fresh bowl of broth, a hunk of bread and a spoon.

She fed him slowly, dunking the bread in the broth so he wouldn't have to chew it, using the spoon to catch the excess dribbling from his lips, and when the bowl was empty he felt strong enough to sit up and lean back against his saddle.

He looked at the woman more carefully than he had before and realized there was more to her than he'd first noticed. Besides being wholesomely pretty, she had a regal quality about her. It surprised him. Since boyhood he'd seen countless women in her position, all of them old before their time, living out their lives of drudgery on ranches just like this and she was the only one who seemed out of place — like a princess in a pig pen, he decided. Despite her earthy, rundown surroundings, cheap cotton dress, worn out shoes and the smudges of dirt on her face, nothing could hide the inner elegance she possessed. It was, he thought, the kind of elegance one could only inherit; the kind that no amount of hardship or adversity could ever destroy. He'd seen it only once before, when in an El Paso barbershop he'd thumbed through an Eastern society magazine and come upon a picture of the British actress, Lily Langtry.

Now she leaned closer, her face swimming in and out of focus. Her lips were moving and her voice broke through his thoughts. 'There's more broth if you want it, mister.'

She had a slight accent. He guessed it was Danish or Swedish and found it pleasing to the ear.

He shook his head. 'Thanks. I'm full.' Seeing his gun-belt lying beside him, he realized she must have put it there while he was asleep and immediately felt secure. The sight of the gun also reminded him of Raven and he asked Ingrid where her daughter was.

'She's out at the corral feeding Brandy.'

'Judas — no!' he exclaimed. 'Don't let her go near that rogue. He — '

' — bites. I know,' Ingrid said ruefully. 'He nipped me when I went to pet him. He also keeps trying to kick down the fence. But with Raven, for some reason he's quite gentle.'

'Don't let him fool you. He's mean to the bone. I've ridden him for five summers and I still wouldn't trust him.'

'I said the same thing to Raven. But she only laughed and said if he's so mean why's he let her rub his nose.'

'Just so's he can take a bigger chunk out of her later. Believe me, ma'am, he will bite her.'

'Well, I'll warn her again,' Ingrid said, rising. 'But I doubt if it'll do any good. She's awfully headstrong. Not even her father could make her do something she didn't want to do, and she adored him.' She picked up the lamp and indicated the little bell beside his saddle. 'If you need anything, just give a ring. I'll leave my window open so I can hear you.'

She went to the double doors. She closed one and was about to close the other when she stopped and looked at him.

'Perhaps tomorrow you'll feel inclined to tell me your name. It's awkward calling you mister all the time.'

He hesitated, reluctant to let anyone know who he was; then sensing he could trust her, said: 'Gabe.'

'Gabe?'

'Short for Gabriel.'

'Oh. And your last name? Raven's too young to address you by your Christian name.'

'Moonlight, ma'am.'

'Gabriel Moonlight.' She considered the name for a moment and nodded approvingly. 'That's very unusual.'

'So is Raven.'

'Yes. I was against calling her that but my husband insisted. Said it was the first thing he thought of when he saw all that shiny black hair and those dark, inquisitive eyes.'

'He's right. Fits.'

'Nevertheless, I would've preferred a more conventional name. Well, good-night, Mr Moonlight. And don't forget: if you need anything just give a ring.' She closed the door — only to open it a second later as he rang the bell.

'Yes?'

''Case it slipped my mind, I'm mighty grateful to you for helpin' me.'

Ingrid smiled, slightly embarrassed. 'It's Raven you should be thanking. She not only found you, but refused to believe me when I said it was too late to save you. She also insisted I let her go to the reservation and beg Almighty Sky to allow Lolotea to come here and bring you back.'

'Make it sound like I was already dead.'

'In my eyes you were.' She thought a

36

moment, still unable to believe what had happened in her barn. 'From now on I'll have more faith in miracles.' She closed the door and he heard her footsteps fading as she walked to the cabin.

It was the last sound he heard before drifting off to sleep.

6

Two more days passed before Gabriel was strong enough to stand; and a third day before he could walk without Ingrid supporting him. During that time, he saw Raven going about her chores. He knew she saw him too, but she wouldn't talk to him or look his way. And once, when she was coming from the barn and he started in her direction, she ran off and refused to answer when he called out to her. He considered talking to Ingrid about her behavior. But he decided this was a personal issue, something to be settled between the two of them, and said nothing to her mother.

On the morning of the fourth day Ingrid met him as he was hobbling back from the corral. He'd been checking on the condition of his horse and had almost gotten bitten for his trouble.

Angered by the Morgan's irascibility he was in no mood to be sociable. But when she invited him to breakfast he managed to be civil and followed her into the cabin.

It smelled of fresh-baked biscuits and hot coffee, neither of which he'd had in a while, and his mood quickly softened.

As he sat at the table and looked around, he realized Raven was absent. Guessing that she'd deliberately avoided him, he smiled to himself and began eating. He devoured a platter of fried eggs, pancakes, crisp bacon and home-made biscuits soaked in gravy and then washed everything down with three mugs of coffee sweetened with canned milk.

'Reckon I was hungrier than I thought,' he said as Ingrid cleared away his dishes.

'I'm glad. I like a man who eats well. It's one of the things I miss most about Sven not being here.'

'Your husband's away, ma'am?'

'He passed on.'

'Sorry. I didn't mean to dig up

unhappy memories.'

'You didn't. My memories of Sven are happy ones.' She paused, wistful, and said: 'We tend to do that, don't we?'

'Do what, ma'am?'

'Remember only the good times?'

He gave a shrug that could have meant anything.

'I mean, when I think of Sven I never think of the times we got cross with each other or argued and went to bed without speaking or — Oh my goodness,' she said, interrupting herself. 'Will you listen to me prattling on? If that isn't so typical of a widow — always living in the past.' She paused, hoping he would pick up the conversation. When he didn't, she guessed he wasn't a man who enjoyed idle chatter. Well, Sven hadn't either, so this was nothing new. Pouring Gabriel another cup of coffee, she set the pot on the stove and went to the window and looked wistfully out at the parched, sunburned landscape.

'If only it would rain.'

'Wouldn't count on it, ma'am.'

'What? Oh . . . no . . . of course not. It is summer after all. But I do so miss the rain.'

'You're not from around here then?'

'Oh, no. Neither was Sven. We were both born in Norway — on the outskirts of Bergen, the gateway to the fjord country. Our families were neighbors and had been friends for generations. When my parents decided to come here it seemed only natural that Sven's did too . . . ' She absently twisted her apronstring around one finger. 'I'm beginning to get used to it now. Sven being gone, I mean. I'll always miss him, of course, but . . . ' She smiled sadly; then after a deep sigh pulled herself together. 'If you care to smoke, Mr Moonlight, I have the makings.'

'Much obliged.'

Ingrid brought him the coffee can containing Sven's tobacco and papers. She then picked up the soap and scrub-brush and began cleaning the stove-top while he rolled a smoke.

'Amazing how time flies. It's been two years and three weeks since my husband was killed. Yet there are still times, even now, when I look around and expect to see him standing there and . . . It's foolish, I know, but I just can't believe he's gone.'

Gabriel felt her pain but said nothing.

'Perhaps it's because of the way he died that I can't get over it.'

Weary, but sensing she needed to talk about it, Gabriel forced himself to ask: 'How'd it happen, ma'am?'

'We — Raven, Sven and I — were in Santa Rosa to pick up supplies and a dress my husband had ordered from St Louis for my birthday. As we were leaving Melvin's Haberdashery, three cowboys came galloping up the street from the Copper Palace — that's a saloon on Lower Front Street in case you haven't been there. They were drunk and hollering at the top of their voices and when they reached Main

Street they started shooting up the town. They weren't trying to hit anyone but folks got scared and began screaming and scattering in all directions and in the chaos one of their bullets . . . happened to hit Sven as he was trying to protect us. I didn't realize he'd been hit at first. Then he collapsed and I saw the blood coming from his head and . . . and by the time I got him to the doctor's office he was . . . was — '

Her words trailed off.

For a few moments all was quiet save for the harsh sound of her brush scrubbing the stove-top.

Then, voice choked with tears, she continued: 'I know that accidents happen . . . that every day folks — decent church-going folks who've done nothing wrong — die just by falling off a wagon or a step-ladder, but . . . oh dear God, why did it have to be Sven? He was such a fine man and such a wonderful father and husband . . . and to have him die this way seems like such a senseless waste.'

Gabriel digested her words.

'The three cowboys, ma'am — what happened to them?'

'Nothing. Oh, they were arrested. There was even a trial and a lot of fancy lawyer talk . . . but when it came to sentencing them, the judge said since no one could prove who fired the actual bullet that killed Sven, that meant it could've come from anywhere and he dismissed all the charges against them.'

Gabriel angrily stubbed out his cigarette. 'Doesn't surprise me. Santa Rosa ain't known as a pillar of justice.'

'You've been there, then?'

'All too often.'

'Then you must've heard of Stillman Stadtlander?'

The name of his former employer, a ruthless, powerful rancher who years ago had falsely accused him of stealing Brandy and turned him into an outlaw, made his blood boil.

'Was he involved in your husband's death, ma'am?'

'Not directly, no. But one of the

cowboys was his son, Slade.'

'And the other two — was it the Iverson brothers?'

'Why, yes. You know them?'

Fighting to keep his composure, he said grimly: 'Heard tell of 'em.'

Before Ingrid could question him further the door was flung open and Raven came hurtling in.

'Momma, Momma — there's men coming! A whole parcel of 'em. Riding this way.'

Gabriel instinctively dropped his hand to his Colt .45. 'Mean a posse?'

'Looks like, yeah.'

'Don't be foolish,' Ingrid said as he got to his feet. 'You can't ride in your condition.'

'Can ride far enough to lead 'em away from here. After that, it won't matter. How far off?' he asked Raven.

'Two miles. Maybe less.'

Ingrid grabbed his arm. 'Wait. I have a better idea.'

'Don't have time to discuss it.'

'Not even if it could save your life?'

Before he could reply she told Raven: 'Take his horse and hide it in Furnace Canyon. Stay with it and keep it quiet till the men are gone.'

'No!' Gabriel pushed Raven aside and turned to Ingrid. 'You want her stomped to death?'

But Raven had already squeezed past him and was sprinting for the corral.

'Goddammit,' he yelled. 'Get back here, girl!'

He limped out of the cabin after her, each step causing a searing pain in his back. 'Y'hear me? Don't go near that damn' sidewinder!'

Raven ignored him. Before he was halfway to the corral, she had opened the gate and swung up onto the stallion's back. The Morgan crouched, like a big cat, and seemed ready to buck her off. But as Raven grabbed its mane and urged it to run, the horse lost its rage and galloped out of the corral.

Stunned, Gabriel watched as Raven, clinging to its back like a limpet, guided the stallion into the scrub-covered hills.

'Come with me,' Ingrid grabbed his arm. 'Hurry.'

She led him to the well. It was surrounded by a low wall and stood at the foot of a makeshift windmill. Lifting the two boards covering the top, she pointed at an iron ladder imbedded in the wall with its bottom half immersed in the water. 'Think you can manage to climb down there?'

He pinned her with his pale blue eyes. 'If they find me, know what they'll do to you?'

'Yes.'

'Dammit, if you won't think of yourself, think of Raven. What her chances will be without you.'

'It took a miracle to save your life,' Ingrid said quietly. 'I'm counting on God not wanting to squander that miracle by deserting us now.' She offered him her hand. 'Ready?'

I was born ready, Gabriel thought. Grasping her hand, he stepped onto the wall, faced her and lowered himself backward down the old, rusty ladder.

Each step sent pain flaring up his back, making him dizzy. Gritting his teeth so he wouldn't cry out, he clung to the rungs and descended into the dark, dank-smelling well.

Ingrid waited until his head was below the wall; then she replaced the boards covering the well and returned to the cabin. There, she picked up a basket of dirty clothes and hurried out to the water trough. She knew she was a poor liar and hoped by keeping busy she would be able to fool whoever questioned her.

7

She was pegging wet clothes to the laundry line when the posse rode in. It was a ragtag bunch made up of two regular deputies and a dozen townsmen temporarily deputized — all led by Stillman Stadtlander's foil, Sheriff Lonnie Forbes.

Ingrid smiled at the tall, big-bellied, gray-mustachioed lawman. 'Good day, Sheriff. What brings you out here?'

'We're huntin' a fella, ma'am.'

Before he could explain further, she told the rest of the posse: 'All of you, back up your horses. I've just washed these clothes and I don't want your dust all over them.'

There was enough annoyance in her voice to make the weary men obey her.

'You could be a tad more sociable, Mrs Bjorkman,' Sheriff Forbes grumbled. 'Boys'n me, we been in the saddle since sunup.'

'And I've been scrubbing and ironing since before that,' Ingrid said tartly. 'But if it's water you need, you're welcome to help yourselves.' She motioned toward the water trough then continued pinning up her laundry.

Telling his men to go ahead, Sheriff Forbes dismounted and asked Ingrid if she'd had any visitors lately.

'Just one.' She spoke with a peg between her teeth and it was difficult to understand her. 'But I don't have to tell you that now, do I? If you hadn't seen his tracks leading in from the desert, you wouldn't have wasted your time coming here.'

The sheriff, who hadn't seen any tracks but wasn't about to admit it, gently took the peg from her mouth.

'This fella we're after, he was here then?'

'I just said that, Sheriff.'

'For how long?'

'Long enough for me to feed him and water his horse.'

'Then, what?'

'He rode off.'

'Just like that?' When she didn't reply, he said: 'Can you describe him?'

'Sure. Tall, lean, lots of dark hair with touches of gray, late thirties, early forties, hard to tell with all the dirt on him; a gunfighter most likely, riding a black horse, a thoroughbred by the look of it — '

'That's the *hombre* all right. Did you patch up his wound, too?'

'There was no need. He'd done that himself. But I did see blood on his shirt. Down here mostly,' she indicated her lower back. 'I knew then he'd been shot. But he didn't favor it much . . . just changed his shirt and went on his way.'

Sheriff Forbes eyed her with barely controlled anger. 'Ever think you might be helpin' an outlaw . . . a murderer on the run?'

'I've already told you he looked like a gunfighter.'

'But you still went ahead an' helped him?'

'I'm a widow with a child. What was I supposed to do? Try to chase him off my property and risk having him shoot me and take what he wanted anyway?'

She had a point, he had to admit. Gazing about him, he said almost sarcastically: 'Don't 'spect he's still here?'

'If he is, then he sneaked back and is hiding somewhere without my knowing.' She pegged up the last sheet, picked up the empty basket and started for the cabin. 'If you think there's a chance of that,' she said as the sheriff fell in beside her, 'I'd appreciate it if you'd have your men look around. I didn't like the way he looked at Raven and I wouldn't want him here when she gets back.'

'Back from where, ma'am?'

'Out there somewhere.' She gestured in the opposite direction to which Raven had ridden off. 'You know how she is, Sheriff. More foot-loose than a coyote. She lit out early this morning. Said she'd seen some Gambel's quail and wanted to snare them for dinner.' Ingrid laughed, hoping it didn't sound forced. 'Truth is, Sheriff, she probably just wanted to get out of helping me do the wash.'

He didn't comment and she couldn't tell if he believed her or not. Shortly, they reached the cabin. She stopped, rested her basket on her hip and faced the big lumbering lawman.

'There's coffee on the stove if you don't mind waiting till I heat it up.'

'Thanks, we gotta keep ridin'. But I will take you up on your offer to look around. You know. Just in case he snuck back without you noticin'.' He rejoined his men and Ingrid, blood running cold, entered the cabin.

At the window she lifted the curtain a little, and watched as the posse searched the property. There wasn't much natural cover and for the most part, the men kept walking. But two stopped by the well. Ingrid held her breath as they spoke and then squinted up at the windmill. Keep moving, she prayed. Please keep moving. One of them must have said something funny because they both laughed and then walked on.

Relieved, Ingrid kept watching.

Presently, several men entered the barn. One of them quickly reappeared and yelled something to the sheriff, who was washing up at the water trough. Quickly knotting his wet kerchief about his neck, he plodded into the barn.

Knowing they must have found traces of Gabriel's blood, Ingrid fought down her fear and went to the stove. Moving the coffee pot over the flame, she stoked the embers and took two mugs out of the cupboard.

'Door's open, Sheriff,' she said when he knocked a few minutes later. Then as he entered: 'Glad you changed your mind. I enjoy company when I'm having my coffee.'

'This ain't about coffee, Mrs Bjorkman. It's 'bout the blood on the floor of your barn.'

'I already told you about that, Sheriff. Remember? I said I knew the man had been shot — '

'So you let him change shirts in your barn?'

'I'm a widow,' Ingrid said indignantly. 'Where would you have him do it — in my bedroom, perhaps?'

Sheriff Forbes went red and stepped back as if stung.

'I meant no offense, ma'am. But I got folks to answer to. Important folks! They expect me to catch this fella, and mighty damn' quick too, and since you're the only person who's seen him since he shot Mr Stadtlander's boy — '

'Slade?' Ingrid said, shocked. 'This man shot Slade Stadtlander?'

'Cut him down right in front of his pa.'

'Dear God, when?'

'Few days ago. And before that, he killed the Iverson brothers. Shot 'em in cold blood outside the Copper Palace.'

Ingrid's mind spun and she gaped at him for a moment. Finally she said: 'I hope you're not expecting me to feel sorry for them. Not when the judge gave them a free pass after they'd killed my husband.'

There was such rage in her blue eyes Sheriff Forbes again stepped back, hands fumbling with the brim of his hat.

'I ain't askin' you to feel any way, Mrs Bjorkman. I'm just tryin' to do my job. Good day to ya.' Turning, he ducked out through the door.

Ingrid quickly sat down before she collapsed. Outside, she heard the sheriff bellowing at his men and shortly after that, saw the posse ride past the window out into the desert.

Then it was all quiet and she was alone. Heart pounding in her ears, she waited long enough to make sure the posse wasn't returning then hurried out to the well.

8

Dusk fell. It came suddenly, silently, covering the desert and surrounding hills like a purple shroud. As if on cue, coyotes started their nightly yipping. Moments later bats appeared, making tiny squeaks as they hunted insects in the darkness. There was still no sign of Raven or the stallion. Ingrid knew Raven knew the desert and its creatures as well as any Apache and tried to convince herself that there was nothing to fear. But as the hours mounted up doubt crept in, especially if her mind happened to dwell on her husband's untimely death, and to stop herself from getting frantic she deliberately kept busy all day. There was the now-dry laundry to be taken down and carefully ironed; the vegetable patch to be weeded; dinner to be fixed; and before any of that, Gabriel's wound to attend to.

Climbing in and out of the well had started it bleeding again and Ingrid, afraid of infection, had insisted he let her bathe it and apply a fresh bandage.

He was a terrible patient. He didn't mention the intense pain she knew he must be feeling, but fussed and grumbled under his breath the whole time she was tending to him.

'My God,' she exclaimed finally. 'Have you never had a woman take care of you before?'

His silence told her he hadn't.

'You've not been wed then?'

He shook his head.

That pleased her, though she was not sure why. 'Surely you've had girl-friends?'

He looked at her, long and hard. 'There's an old Apache saying — '

' 'It's impolite to ask a direct question', yes, I'm well aware of it. But we aren't Apaches, Mr Moonlight. We're civilized human beings. And since you're staying with us and I know nothing about you — '

'One,' he admitted grudgingly, 'a long time ago.'

'What was she like?'

Gabriel reflected a moment, searching for words to describe the woman he'd once loved. Time had dimmed his memory of her but he could still recall how Cally Kincaide looked as she stood in the doorway of her cantina in Santa Rosa, untamed and beautiful, trying not to cry as she watched him ride off only minutes ahead of a pursuing posse. Then it came to him and with a wry smile, he said:

'Raven — ten years down the trail.'

Ingrid laughed. 'She must've been a handful. What happened to her?'

He would have preferred to drop the subject. But there was something about this woman, a feeling of genuine warmth and caring that overrode his normally quiet, taciturn demeanor and he heard himself saying: 'She was raped an' . . . killed.'

Ingrid gave a tiny gasp and bit her knuckle. 'Dear God, how awful. Did they catch the men who did it?'

'Yeah,' he said bitterly. 'But like with your man, they weaseled their way out of it.'

She shook her blonde head in disgust. 'Makes you wonder if there's any justice in the world, doesn't it?'

'I pack my justice with me,' he said grimly.

For a second she didn't understand. Then she saw the six-shooter on his hip and said: ''Mean, you killed them?'

She saw her answer in his narrowed, flint-blue eyes.

'Is that how you got shot in the back?'

He nodded.

'Who did it — Slade or one of the Iversons?'

Gabriel frowned. 'Sheriff tell you that?'

'Yes. Only I'm sure his version of what happened is different than yours.'

'Any way you cut it, they're still dead.'

'And you're wanted for murder,' she reminded.

Outside, a rider approached. Gabriel

drew his Colt — so quickly it seemed to leap into his hand. He went to blow out the lamp on the table. But Ingrid, already at the window, stopped him. 'It's Raven.'

Together, they hurried outside.

'Where've you been?' Ingrid said as her daughter slid off the Morgan's back. 'Sheriff Forbes and his men have been gone for hours.'

'I wanted to make sure they weren't coming back.' Raven looked at Gabriel, who was studying the stallion. 'I didn't run him into the ground, if that's what you're thinking.'

'I can see that.' Gabriel stepped closer to get a better look at the Morgan — only to jerk back as the horse tried to bite him. Wincing from the pain shooting up his back, he said sourly: 'Too bad you didn't. Might've gotten rid of some of his orneriness.'

'He's not ornery, mister. Just feisty.'

'Raven, what have I told you about contradicting your elders?'

'But it's true, Momma.' She brushed

her shiny black hair out of her face. 'In all the time I was with him he never once tried to bite me.'

'He will,' Gabriel warned. 'Sure as night falls, he will.' He slapped the Morgan on the rump with his old campaign hat. Startled, the horse tried to kick him then trotted into the corral.

'Maybe if you didn't beat on him all the time,' Raven said, closing the gate, 'he wouldn't be so quick to retaliate. Ever think of that?'

'Every second of every day,' Gabriel said sarcastically. Rolling his eyes at Ingrid, he limped off to the barn.

Raven glared after him. 'If that's all the thanks I get for saving his neck, next time he can go hide his horse himself!'

'Hush, child. That's no way to talk. Besides, I'm sure Mr Moonlight appreciates what you did.'

'Well, he's got a damn funny way of showin' it — '

'Watch your tongue, young lady, or I'll wash your — ' She broke off as

Raven ran into the cabin.

About to follow her, Ingrid paused in the doorway and gazed at the barn. Lamplight showed through the chinks in the boards. In her mind she saw Gabriel stretched out on the straw, head resting on his saddle, smoking Sven's tobacco . . .

The thought of her late husband made her feel lonely, and suddenly she had a strange yearning to join Gabriel. Shocked and at the same time titillated by her feelings for a stranger, a man who in almost every way was the exact opposite of Sven, she scolded herself for having such lascivious thoughts and hurried indoors to give Raven her supper.

9

Gabriel awakened just before sunup the next morning. The pain in his lower back was less excruciating and he knew now he could tolerate it. Pulling on his boots, he gently stretched the stiffness from his muscles then left the barn and walked slowly to the water trough.

The sun was still below the eastern horizon, while overhead a sliver of moon still lingered in the cloudy, lavender-gray sky. A cool, dry breeze off the desert washed over his face, tugging at his unruly black hair. He took a deep breath, filling his lungs with the fragrance of candlewood and desert lilies, and expelled it in a long deep sigh of satisfaction.

For the first time in three days he felt truly alive. Ever since he had ridden away from Cally's sister, Ellen, who had begged him to let her take him to a doctor, he'd expected to die. He had hung on for as long as he could, all sense of time and reality suspended in his mind. But as his life-blood slowly drained from him, saturating his shirt and reddening the flanks of the Morgan, he'd gradually lost consciousness.

But every man has a time to die and this hadn't been Gabriel's. And now, thanks to strangers, here he was, alive and on the mend.

As he bent over the trough he saw the moon floating on the surface of the water. He playfully poked it with his finger and the reflection dissolved into shimmering ripples. Splashing cold water on his face, he straightened up and patted himself dry with his kerchief.

High overhead, a hawk screeched. He looked up and saw it, wings outspread, drifting on a thermal as it searched the desert for breakfast.

Off to his left the circular vane of the old, patched wind-mill creaked in the wind above the well. It reminded him of yesterday, of how the woman's quick thinking had saved his life a second time, and he looked at the cabin, hoping to see Ingrid standing in the door beckoning him in for breakfast. But the door was closed and no light showed inside. Glumly, he realized he'd have to wait a little longer for his coffee.

As he walked to the barn he heard a familiar snorting behind him, followed by pounding hoofs. Whirling, he looked at the corral — in time to see the Morgan charging toward the fence. A collision seemed inevitable. But at the last instant the stallion leaped, effortlessly clearing the fence. It landed and without breaking stride charged toward him. Its teeth were bared and there was red fire in its eyes and Gabriel knew the horse intended to run him down.

There was nowhere to hide and in his condition it was useless to try and run; so Gabriel stood there, wishing he hadn't left his Colt in the barn, watching the stallion rushing at him.

'C'mon, you black devil,' he yelled at

it. 'Do your goddamn worst!'

The stallion was almost on him now. Gabriel felt the ground trembling underfoot. He tensed himself for the blow. But it never came. At the last instant the charging Morgan swerved, narrowly missing Gabriel, its body so close that its flowing tail whipped him across the chest.

Relieved, and at the same time angered by the stallion's erratic behavior, Gabriel watched it stop a short distance past him. He expected it to charge him again. Instead it reared up, front legs pawing at the air and whinnied triumphantly — as if, Gabriel thought, to remind him who was really the boss.

'I knew he was foolin' with you,' a small voice said.

Gabriel turned and saw Raven approaching from the desert, slingshot in one hand and two dead rabbits in the other.

'That so? Know all about horses, do you?'

'Not all,' she said, unfazed by his sarcasm. 'But enough to know a bluff when I see one.'

'Maybe you'd feel a mite different if you were standin' right in front him.'

'I doubt it,' she said brashly. 'Brandy tried to ramrod me for a spell yesterday while we were hiding in Furnace Canyon. But once he saw I wasn't gonna get riled up like you do, he soon got his manners back. Did you know he likes piñon nuts?' she added. 'Well, he does. Lots. In fact if I was you, mister, I'd fill my pockets with 'em and then maybe you'd be able to win him over like I did.'

Gabriel was tempted to hold her over his knee and spank the daylights out of her.

Raven, sensing she'd gone too far, got ready to take off. 'Had a dog like him once,' she said. 'A Mescalero named Two Bears gave him to me. Well, that ain't entirely true. Apaches were gonna eat him so I stole him 'fore they could. But you think that mutt was grateful?

Heck, no. Used to growl and snap at me whenever I got too close. I took a switch to him a few times but it only made him worse. Got so I almost quit taking him hunting with me — '

'If you're tryin' to make a point,' Gabriel broke in irritably, 'now'd be the time to get to it.'

'He saved my life, that's the point, mister. Got himself all tore up by a mountain lion just to give me time to run away.'

'Brave dog, all right. But with Brandy you're mistaking courage for meanness. He wouldn't fight a mountain lion for me. He'd sooner watch me get all chewed up.'

'That so?' Raven said in the same tone he'd used earlier. 'Well, if that's how you figure it, mister, reckon there's no use in me telling you 'bout how many miles he carried you without water when you was all shot up . . . or how many buzzards he kept from pecking your guts out till Momma an' me got back with the wagon. No sirree.

I mean I'm just a runt of a girl. Wouldn't be right for me to tell a growed man how wrong he was, now would it?' Whistling insolently, she walked off to the cabin.

'Hold up, missy.'

Raven turned and saw respect had replaced the anger in Gabriel's pale blue eyes.

'I'm obliged to you for bringin' that to my attention. Some times even a 'growed man' gets to thinking so much 'bout himself he forgets how much he owes others around him.' With a tip of his hat, he headed back to the barn.

'Wait . . . ' Raven, impressed by his response, held the dead rabbits up by their ears. 'Wanna help me skin these?'

'Only if I get to help you eat 'em.'

'Deal.'

* * *

That night they ate rabbit stew for supper. Ingrid flavored it with onions or 'skunk eggs' as Gabriel called them, carrots, potatoes and herbs, all from her garden, and as an extra treat whipped up flour dumplings. She also intended to bake a pie. But Raven surprised her by offering to make one for her — 'You got so much else to do, Momma.'

'Well, thank you, lamb. That would be most helpful.' Ingrid, not fooled by her daughter's unusual eagerness to help, got an even bigger surprise when just before Gabriel arrived Raven walked out of the bedroom with her hair brushed and wearing her one and only Sunday dress. It had been so long since Ingrid had seen her in anything but frayed jeans and a soiled boy's shirt that her mouth fell open.

'Why you gaping at me like that?' Raven demanded. 'It's nothing but a silly old gingham dress.'

'And very pretty you look in it, too. I'm sure Mr Moonlight will be delighted — '

'I'm not wearing it for him, Momma. I just felt like putting it on is all. So don't go making a big fuss out of it.'

There was a knock on the half-open door and Gabriel poked his head in. 'Hope I'm not too early,' he said when Ingrid beckoned him in. 'But the smell of that pie baking got my mouth to waterin' — ' He stopped, surprised, as he saw Raven in her primrose dress and then turned to Ingrid. 'You didn't tell me you were invitin' a lady to supper.'

'That's because I wasn't aware of it myself,' she said, smiling. 'Puts us all to shame, doesn't she?'

'All right,' Raven scowled. 'Dang it, that's enough. You two can quit your teasing now or I'm gonna take this dumb thing off.'

'Why, bless me, it's Raven,' Gabriel deadpanned. 'I never would've guessed.'

'I'm warning you, mister.'

'Now, now,' Ingrid soothed. 'That's enough. Let's all be nice and polite and sit down to supper. But I feel obliged to tell you,' she added to Gabriel. 'The berry pie you mentioned — I didn't bake it. Raven did.'

Gabriel arched his brows, impressed.

'Well, ain't you a daisy. Territory's full of pretty women but a pretty woman who can bake a pie smells like that — now that's a rare commodity an' somethin' a fella would find hard to resist.'

Raven blushed, murmured 'good-God-almighty' under her breath and ran into the bedroom.

Amused, Ingrid whispered to Gabriel. 'I fear she has a crush on you.'

'I'm flattered. But I don't want her missin' supper over it.'

Ingrid motioned for him to remain seated and entered the bedroom. Shortly she reappeared, pushing Raven ahead of her.

'Now,' she said when they were all seated. 'Perhaps you'd be kind enough to lead us in prayer, Mr Moonlight.'

'My pleasure, ma'am. And please, call me Gabe.'

10

By the end of the week Gabriel, though still sore, had healed enough to help Ingrid and Raven gather vegetables from the patch beside the cabin. When that task was finished and Raven had gone off to hunt quail, he offered to make a few much-needed repairs to the corral fence, barn and cabin.

Ingrid thanked him but said it wasn't necessary. She had already sold the ranch to Mr Lylo Willis, who ran the telegraph office in Santa Rosa, and because of its rundown condition had accepted a lower price than it was worth.

Surprised, Gabriel asked her when she and Raven were moving.

'End of this month. We're going to live with my step-brother, Reece, in California. He's been nagging me to come ever since Sven died. But I couldn't bring myself to leave here.' She looked sadly about her. 'This is all I have left to remember him by . . . and it's taken me this long to find the will to pull up stakes and go on without him.'

Wondering why it mattered to him if she or her daughter left or not, Gabriel said: 'How's Raven feel about movin'?'

'She's undecided . . . changes her mind from day to day. She loves the desert and the freedom it gives her, but at the same time she's excited about going somewhere new and living in a big fine house with servants — '

'Your stepbrother's fared well, then?'

'Very well. Reece owns the town bank, a general store and from what he says in his letters a lot of land as well.'

'Then you shouldn't want for anything.'

'Absolutely not. He's made that very clear. Says I won't have to lift a finger. He's also made plans for Raven to attend a school for fine young ladies in Sacramento.'

The idea amused Gabriel and he

couldn't help grinning.

'I know what you're thinking and I felt the same way. Poor Reece has no idea what a handful she is and, frankly, I haven't let on. I know that's dishonest but, well, there's always the chance that once she gets there and settles in, she'll change. People do, you know,' Ingrid added when he frowned. 'I know in Raven's case it's hard to believe — '

'That's not what was on my mind, ma'am. I was thinkin' that if she was my daughter I wouldn't want her to. I'd want her to stay just like she is. Not often you find a young'un with her kind of savvy an' grit.'

'Heavens, now you sound like my husband — that's exactly what he would have said.' She paused, troubled by her thoughts. 'Sven didn't like my brother much. He only met Reece a few times, but he formed a bad opinion of him. And whenever I tried to defend him, Sven would accuse me of turning a blind eye. We seldom argued about anything, but when it came to Reece we disagreed vehemently. I can remember Sven saying to me once: 'For God's sake, woman, open your eyes and see this man for what he really is — a greedy, ruthless land baron who'll stop at nothing to get what he wants!' Of course, that was just his opinion, and a very biased opinion at that — '

'Biased?'

'Reece didn't want me to marry Sven. He thought he was a good man, but felt financially I could do better. In fact he was angry at me when I ignored his advice and married Sven. Said I'd rue the day.'

'Did you?'

'Never. Not once, not even for a second. But somehow Sven found out about what Reece said and never forgave him. Which was sad. Though Reece is only my stepbrother, he's always done his best to take care of me. I love him very much and because of the rift that sprang up between him and Sven, I was forced to make a choice — my husband or Reece. As a result, we didn't see each other for several years.'

'An' now you'n Raven are gonna go live with him.'

'Sounds like you think I'm making a mistake.'

'Wasn't my intention.'

'Well, I'm not,' Ingrid said adamantly. 'I admit Reece can be pugnacious and difficult to deal with at times, like any businessman . . . and he does enjoy getting his own way. But he's not ruthless and he's not greedy. He's generous. In fact he's one of the most generous men I've ever known.'

To Gabriel, it sounded like she was trying to convince herself that her step-brother was a fine man and instinctively he wondered why.

Misunderstanding his silence, she said: 'My goodness, listen to me carrying on. Forgive me. I usually don't burden other people with my problems. But I can't discuss this with Raven. She's far too young to understand any of it — '

'It's no burden, ma'am. Everyone needs to talk to somebody.'

'I've noticed you don't.'

'Maybe I've been alone too long.'

'Oh, I'm not criticizing. In fact I'm envious. I'd give anything not to be so needy, so dependent upon the love and affection of others — ' She broke off, embarrassed, and then only half-teasingly said: 'Perhaps I should have you teach me how to be a gunfighter . . . then I could be as independent and free as you.'

'Guns don't bring independence, ma'am. Or freedom. Truth is they can sometimes keep a fella boxed up.'

'Then why do you keep using them?'

'Don't have much choice.'

'Because of your reputation?'

His tight-lipped silence answered her question.

'What if you went somewhere else, some place far away where no one knows you?'

'An' do what? Tend bar in a cantina? Sell dresses an' nails in a general store?

Wear a badge for fifty an' found till some saddle tramp sees a wanted poster an' puts one in my back? For gunfighters . . . life ain't long on options.'

The stress of the past few days showed on his weary, rugged face and her heart went out to him. Moving close, she rested her hands on his shoulders and looked up into his light blue eyes.

'If by some miracle you could hang up your guns — would you?'

'I don't deal in miracles,' he said. 'I deal in lead.'

It was not the answer she'd hoped for. She stepped back, upset by his response, and started for the cabin.

He knew he'd hurt her and cursed himself for letting his anger get the better of him. For a moment he considered calling her back and explaining that five years ago Cally had asked him the same thing. Younger then and still filled with hope, he'd answered yes. Encouraged, she had ignored public opinion and a warning from the territorial marshal, and become his woman. And from then on her life had been a living hell.

Not about to put another caring woman through the same anguish, he waited until Ingrid reached the cabin then said quietly: 'Reckon I'll be ridin' on tomorrow.'

'Tomorrow?' She turned back to him, making no effort to hide her dismay. 'But, why? What's your hurry?'

'No hurry. Figure it's time.'

'I wish you'd reconsider, Gabe.' When he didn't reply, she added: 'It would mean a lot to me if you'd stay on until Raven and I leave for California. It's only another week or so.'

'Why till then?'

'Well, for one thing you'd be completely healed. You start riding too soon and you might reopen your wound. And once it starts bleeding again it could get infected — '

'What's the other reason?'

She hesitated.

'If you want me to stay, ma'am, I gotta know why.'

'It's Raven. Before you showed up she was giving me fits. She fought me over everything — refused to do anything I asked and threw tantrums whenever I put my foot down. I thought at first it was just her age and rebellious nature. But as time wore on I realized it went much deeper.'

He waited, wondering how that involved him.

She seemed to read his mind. 'Raven likes you. More importantly, she respects you. You're a man and right now she needs a man to look up to.'

'Ma'am — '

'No, no, please listen. Although Raven's never come right out and said it, I know she blames me for Sven's death and ever since that day has seemed intent on making my life miserable. But now, with you around, she seems to have gotten over all that and become her old self again.'

He thought a moment before asking:

'Why you? You didn't pull the trigger.'

'In her eyes I might just as well have. She believes if we hadn't gone to Melvin's Haberdashery to pick up my birthday dress, her father wouldn't have gotten shot. I've tried to talk her out of it, but she won't listen. She's convinced herself that I'm to blame and that's all there is to it.'

He slowly digested her words. 'How 'bout you?'

'Do I think I'm to blame?' Ingrid shrugged, dejected. 'At this stage I don't know what to think. No, that's not true. Yes. Occasionally. When I'm feeling really low. Then doubt creeps in and I start wondering. I mean, I surely didn't need a fancy new dress, not living way out here. Yet I went ahead and helped Sven pick it out of the catalogue . . . chose the day we rode into town and — ' Her voice trailed off and tears glinted in her cornflower eyes.

Feeling uncomfortable, as he always did when women cried around him, Gabriel wished he was better with words so he could soothe her and make her understand that death didn't work that way. It didn't play favorites; once it chose its victim nothing could swerve it from its course.

'Want me to talk to her?'

'Thank you, no. She might think I put you up to it and then she'd hate me even more.'

Gabriel shifted uncomfortably.

Seeing how ill at ease he was, Ingrid dried her eyes on her apron, said: 'I'm sorry I imposed on you like that. It was wrong of me. You're not responsible for Raven or me — '

'But I am indebted to you.'

'Nonsense. We did no more than any other civilized person would do under the circumstances.'

'I'll stay,' he said quietly.

'No, no, I won't hear of it — '

'And I'll ride with you to Las Cruces — that's where you're catchin' the train to California, right?'

'Yes, but — well, thank you, but I wouldn't dream of putting you to that sort of inconvenience.'

'No inconvenience. I'm goin' there anyways.'

'You sure? You're not just saying that to make me feel better?'

'No. There's a lady I know at the mission. She means a lot to me and I want her to know I'm still alive.'

Ingrid felt a twinge of jealousy but quickly dismissed it. 'So, there is a woman in your life?'

Before he could reply, they heard Raven yelling outside.

'Rider comin'!'

Gabriel and Ingrid exchanged uneasy glances and then hurried out to the corral.

'Over there,' Raven pointed to the north. 'He's too far off to see who it is, but I reckoned you'd want to know.'

She was speaking to Gabriel. He nodded his thanks then asked her to get his field glasses from his saddle-bags.

'Most likely he's heading for Santa Rosa,' Ingrid said as Raven ran to the barn. 'Maybe even the border.'

Gabriel didn't say anything. But his gut instinct said this rider wasn't a good omen.

Shortly Raven returned, gave him his glasses and pointed out into the desert. 'See . . . there . . . just to the left of that butte.'

Removing the glasses from the old traveling case, he blew on the lenses, wiped them clean with his sleeve cuff and focused them on the approaching rider.

'It's a man, all right. On a grullo. Got his hat pulled down low so's I can't see his face. But he's ridin' like a man who's got all day to get where he's goin'.'

'May I look?' Ingrid said. 'Maybe there's something about him or his horse I'll recognize.'

He handed her the glasses. She trained them on the rider then shook her head and said he didn't look familiar.

'I wonder who he is?'

'Bounty hunter, most likely.'

'What makes you say that?'

'A cowboy's got no need for more'n a Winchester and a pistol. This fella's packin' two on the hip, a belly gun an' a Sharps-Borchardt rifle, Model 1878 in his saddle boot.'

'You can tell all that from here?'

'Bein' observant, it's what keeps a man alive.'

'Maybe he won't stop here,' Raven said hopefully. 'Maybe he'll circle 'round us and keep riding?'

'Anything's possible.' Gabriel focused the glasses on the rider again. There was something familiar about the erect, cocky way he sat in the saddle and the matching ivory-grip .44s poking from his black-leather, tied-down holsters that raised a question mark in Gabriel's memory — and as the man suddenly looked up, showing his face, he realized why:

'Damn,' he said softly.

'You know him?' Raven said.

'Latigo Rawlins — yeah, I know him.'

'Sounds as if you don't like him much.'

'He's a shootist,' Gabriel said as if that answered her question. 'A hired gun.' Catching her 'like you?' look, he added: 'He kills folks for money.'

'Is he fast?'

'Still alive, ain't he?'

'Faster'n you?'

'Raven,' her mother began crossly.

'I'm just asking, Momma.'

'Hopefully,' Gabriel said to Raven, 'I'll never find that out.'

'Do you think he's coming here after you?' Ingrid asked. 'I mean, could Mr Stadtlander have hired him?'

'Anything's possible,' Gabriel repeated. He took another look through the glasses at the rider then walked off.

They watched him enter the barn. When he reappeared a few moments later he'd buckled on his gun-belt and was tying the holster down, gunfighter-style. As he joined them he drew his Peacemaker, spun the cylinder across his forearm to make sure the gun was fully loaded, and then slid the Colt back into its well-oiled holster.

'Take Raven inside,' he told Ingrid. 'An' stay there till I tell you to come out.'

Ingrid didn't move. 'This gunman, Latigo whatever his name is, he won't be here for at least another ten or fifteen minutes. That's more than enough time for you to saddle up and go wait in the hills till he's gone.'

'Runnin' ain't the answer.'

'I'll go with you,' Raven offered. 'Show you where to hide.'

Gabriel shook his head. 'I need to get this settled. Now do like I say, ma'am.'

Grudgingly, Ingrid led Raven into the cabin. But by the way she slammed the door he knew she was angry with him.

11

Gabriel rolled a smoke, flared a match to it and sat on the edge of the water trough. He made sure the sun was behind him, and in the face of the rider, and then watched Latigo Rawlins riding toward him.

He'd first met the little Texan in the Acme Saloon in El Paso, the same saloon in which lawman John Selman would eventually shoot the notorious John Wesley Hardin in the back of the head. That night Gabriel and Latigo had faced each other across a poker table. Neither lost nor won much, and afterward they talked over drinks at the bar. Their meeting didn't turn into a friendship; but during their conversation they discovered they had several things in common. Both were loners. Both had lost their parents while still in their mid teens. And both had a reputation for settling disputes with their guns.

During the ensuing years they had occasionally run into each other in various towns across the southwest and though they'd never had to confront one another, accounts of their individual exploits forced them to grudgingly respect each other's speed with a gun.

Many people, especially lawmen, considered them cut from the same cloth and hoped they would kill each other off. Because of Latigo's immense ego it probably would have happened too; but before the big showdown could take place Gabriel was branded a horse-thief by Stillman Stadtlander and forced to flee to Mexico.

Now, as Latigo Rawlins drew close enough to recognize Gabriel, the small, handsome, sandy-haired shootist reined in his horse, removed his cigarette and whistled softly. 'I'll be damned. Is that really you, Mesquite?'

'Mesquite Jennings is dead,' Gabriel said, referring to the name he'd used when he had first become an outlaw. 'He was shot down by the *Rurales* south of the border.'

Latigo Rawlins chewed on Gabriel's words a moment, then said: 'Then who might I be talkin' to now?'

'Gabe Moonlight.'

'Whooeee. That's mighty fancy.'

'It's my natural born name.'

'True?'

'True.'

'Hell, I never knew that.' Latigo had a boyish voice to go with his boyish grin. 'All these years, amigo, an' you never once mentioned it.'

'Had no call to.'

That seemed to satisfy Latigo. He took a long drag on his cigarette and flicked the butt away. 'I heard a story once. Don't recall who told me but they said you took the name Mesquite Jennings from of one of them dime novels. That so?'

'Yep.'

'Why'd you kill it off?'

'It'd worn out its welcome.'

'Too bad. Me, I always liked the sound of it. Had flair. Like a woman in red satin and black knickers.' He twisted slowly in the saddle trying to stretch the stiffness from his back. 'Sure 'preciate it if I could step down and water my horse.'

'Help yourself.' Gabriel watched as the little gunfighter dismounted. He did it in one slow fluid movement, making sure his hands were always near his guns, and led his horse to the trough.

'That's a fine lookin' grullo,' Gabriel said as the leggy, mouse-colored dun buried its muzzle in the water.

'Won it from a fella in a cantina in Alamogordo. Bluffed him into foldin' with just one deuce showin'.'

'Still playin' stud then?'

'Every chance I get. You?'

'Not so much.'

'Bein' on the run'll do that to a fella.' Latigo laughed mirthlessly. Then removing his hat, he slapped the trail dust from it against his leathers, dipped it into the trough and poured water over his head. 'I was due for a new pony, anyway. My roan was all wore out.'

He drank from his cupped hands, ran his dripping fingers through his curly fair hair and dried them off on his denim shirt. Then sitting beside Gabriel, he took out the makings and rolled himself a smoke.

'Any time you feel like it,' he said, scratching a match on his thumbnail, 'you can tell them two women it's safe to come out now.'

Gabriel looked at the grullo and noticed the tip of a brass nautical spyglass poking out of the saddle-bags. 'They're doin' fine where they are. 'Sides, you ain't gonna be here that long.'

Latigo grinned wryly. 'No. Didn't think I would be.' His eyes, yellow as firelight, settled on Gabriel for an instant and in that instant Gabriel felt a cold chill run up his spine. It wasn't fear, he knew; just an instinct warning him never to draw on this man unless he had an edge.

Rising, Latigo lazily stepped into the

saddle and backed the grullo up without his eyes ever leaving Gabriel. 'Thanks for the water, *amigo*.'

Gabriel nodded, ready to slap leather if Latigo even looked like he was going to draw.

But the little shootist made no attempt to go for his gun. Instead, once he was a few yards away he reined up, leaned on his saddle horn and gave Gabriel a cold smile.

'If you ever get a hankerin' to put distance 'tween you and here, look me up in California. I'll be up north in Old Calico. Could be I'll need someone like you.'

'To do what?'

'Watch my back. Man I'm gonna work for says the last two guns he hired were dry-gulched.'

'I'll think on it, Lefty.'

Latigo chuckled. 'Been a spell since anyone called me that. Adios!' He wheeled the grullo around and dug his spurs in, launching the startled horse into a gallop.

Gabriel breathed easier and signaled to the cabin. The curtains stirred and moments later Ingrid and Raven came out.

'What did he want?' Raven asked.

'Was he after you?' Ingrid added.

'Hard to tell,' Gabriel said. 'Claimed he's on his way to work for some fella in Old Calico, but — '

'Old Calico?' Ingrid said, surprised.

'You've heard of it?'

'That's where my stepbrother lives. It's a small town in the gold country near Placerville. What a coincidence.'

'Maybe he's gonna work for Uncle Reece?' Raven said.

'Don't be silly. What use would he have for a shootist?' She turned back to Gabriel. 'How would this Latigo know you're here? No one else does.'

'Don't figure he did. Not at first. But he's got one of them fancy sea-captain's spyglasses so he might've seen me from way off on that butte an' decided to get a closer look. By now Stadtlander must've put a reward out for me, an'

Latigo, he was born with a nose for blood money.'

'Does that mean he'll be back?'

'I doubt it,' Gabriel said. 'Latigo plays life like he plays poker — bluffing losers. Now that he's seen I'm not all shot up like maybe he heard, he's most likely to use that Sharps of his to gun me down from long range.'

'Mean he'll bushwhack you?' Raven said.

'Mean he'll try.'

'Dear God,' Ingrid said. 'This is the nineteenth century. Aren't we ever going to learn to get along with one another?'

12

The rest of the week passed uneventfully. Raven, delighted that Gabriel was accompanying them to Las Cruces, was on her best behavior and did all she could to be helpful. She fetched water for her mother, hung clothes out to dry, swept the cabin and even finished the reading and arithmetic lessons that Ingrid composed for her — all without complaint.

She also tried to be around Gabriel as much as possible, fetching things for him, sewing buttons on his shirts, and offering to groom the stallion so that he didn't have to risk re-injuring his healed wound.

Ingrid, though accustomed to mercurial mood swings in Raven's personality, was nonetheless astounded by the change in her daughter.

'If I hadn't seen it with my own eyes,'

she remarked to Gabriel, 'I wouldn't have believed it possible. Thanks to you, she's turned into a little angel.'

He was skeptical. Though he enjoyed Raven's company, he felt uneasy about the way she fawned over him when they were alone. Occasionally he caught her staring at him with such intensity it made him uncomfortable. He sensed there was more behind her adoration than she let on, and was worried that her 'crush' might develop into something more than he could handle. But when he mentioned it to Ingrid she only laughed and assured him that it was a perfectly normal reaction: all young girls had crushes, she said. It was part of growing up. Why, she herself had mooned over her neighbor's son while growing up, and when he and his family moved away she was convinced her heart was permanently broken.

Having no prior experience with teenage girls, Gabriel accepted her explanation and said no more. He wasn't sold, but he just decided not to worry about it. In two more days they were leaving for Las Cruces and once he put them on the train, he'd never see either of them again.

Raven, however, had no intention of losing Gabriel. For days now, while busy with her chores, she had been trying to think of a way to keep everyone together. Finally, on the night before they departed, she made a point of helping her mother pack the few personal belongings they were taking with them just so she could be alone with her.

'Momma, know what I wish?'

'No, lamb. What?'

'I wish Gabe was coming with us to Old Calico.'

'Mr Moonlight to you, young lady.'

'But he told me to call him Gabe.'

'I don't care what he told you. You know better than to address your elders by their first names. As for your wish, dear, I wouldn't get your hopes up. I very much doubt if he will change his mind.'

'But you wouldn't mind if he did, would you?'

'N-no . . . I suppose not. Ridiculous as it sounds after such a short time, I've grown used to having Mr Moonlight around. I'd enjoy his company — not to mention his protection — on such a long journey.'

'Why don't you ask him then?'

'Ask him what — to come with us? Oh, no, I couldn't possibly do that.'

'Why not?'

'It would be much too forward of me. It not only would embarrass him but it'd be very awkward for both of us.'

'Why?'

'Well, for one thing he has a lady friend in Las Cruces.'

'No, that's not true!'

'But it is. He told me so himself.'

'When?'

'The other day, when he offered to accompany us to the train station.'

'I don't believe you.'

'Believe what you like. It's still true. She's at the mission . . . waiting for him, I presume.'

'Liar!'

'How dare you!' Ingrid went to slap Raven but at the last moment controlled herself and lowered her hand. 'Now apologize, this instant.'

'Why should I? I ain't the one making up stories.'

'Neither am I. And don't say ain't. Why would I make up a story like that?' she added, as Raven sulked.

'So you don't have to ask him to come with us.'

'That's ridiculous. I've already said I'd like him to come.'

'Then I'll ask him.'

'You'll do no such thing. It's not your place. Now stop being foolish and help me carry these valises into the other room.'

Sullenly, Raven obeyed. But as she set her mother's old worn suitcase down by the door, tears welled in her eyes and she said suddenly: 'I hate him.'

'Don't be ridiculous. 'Course you don't hate him — '

'Do, too. Wish now I'd never helped him when he was dying.'

'Shame on you! That's a dreadful thing to say.'

'I don't care. It's how I feel. An' I'm never gonna change my mind, so there!' She stormed from the cabin.

★ ★ ★

Gabriel was perched on the corral fence watching the stallion prance around when Raven ran past. Noticing that she was crying he called out to her. She ignored him and kept running. He called out again, louder this time, and again she ignored him. Puzzled, he watched her get swallowed up by the darkness. Wondering why she was so upset, he climbed down and went to the cabin.

Ingrid answered his knock and invited him.

'What's wrong with Raven?'

Before answering, she poured them both a cup of coffee and sat across the table from him.

'Why? Was she rude to you?'

'No. But she was bawlin' like a sick calf an' took off into the desert.'

'It's nothing. She's just upset about something I said and as usual has gone off to sulk.'

'Was it about me?'

Ingrid hesitated, loath to reveal Raven's problem. Then deciding no harm could come from it, she explained what happened.

Gabriel didn't answer. Rolling himself a smoke from Sven's makings that he now kept in a pouch in his pocket, he licked the paper, flared a match and exhaled a lungful of smoke toward the ceiling.

'I don't blame you for being angry with me,' Ingrid said, misunderstanding his silence. 'I'd no right to reveal something personal that was told me in confidence, but — '

'I'm not angry,' he said. 'An' what I told you wasn't in confidence. Fact is I was hopin' that when we got to Las Cruces you'n Raven would come to the mission with me. I'd like you to meet Ellie. An' I'm sure she'd enjoy meetin' you.'

Ingrid felt the same twinge of jealousy she'd felt previously. Controlling it, she said: 'That's her name — Ellie?'

'Ellen — Ellen Kincaide, yeah.'

'If there's time before our train leaves, I'd love to meet her.' Ingrid smiled without humor. 'It might be better all around if Raven waits in the wagon, though — considering her crush on you and how unpredictable she is.'

'No,' Gabriel said firmly, 'it's important Raven meet her too.'

'Why's that, if I may ask?'

'It'll ease her mind.' Stubbing out his cigarette, he went to the door. Pausing, he looked at her with a trace of regret. 'See, Ellie's got her heart set on bein' a nun. An' though she's got feelings for me, God's corralled all her love.' He left, the door banging shut behind him.

Rising, Ingrid went to the window and stared out after him. Her heart was pounding. She knew it was ridiculous to care for a man she hardly knew — worse, a gunfighter wanted by the law — but she couldn't control her emotions. Nor did she want to. For the first time since losing Sven, she realized she cared about a man and felt whole again.

13

That night Gabriel was sound asleep in his bedroll when Ingrid knocked on the barn door. 'It's me, Gabe. Don't shoot.'

Gabriel lowered the hammer on his Colt. 'Come in.'

The door creaked open and Ingrid entered. She wore a robe over her white nightgown and carried a kerosene lamp. 'I'm sorry to wake you, but I'm worried. Raven hasn't come home and it's way past midnight.'

'Damn.'

'She's never stayed out all night before — '

'Meet me by the corral. Go, woman,' he said when she lingered. 'Longer you stand there, longer I can't get my duds on.'

Within minutes Gabriel joined Ingrid at the corral gate. A full moon was all the light he needed to saddle the stallion.

'I want to go with you, Gabe.'

'No.'

'But I know all the places Raven hides.'

'An' she knows you know an' those are the places she won't be.' Mounting, he leaned down and cupped her chin in his hand, tilting her face up until he could see the reflection of the moon in her eyes. 'Don't worry. I'll find her. Got my word on it.'

★ ★ ★

As the Morgan galloped out into the moonlit desert, Gabriel ignored the twinges of pain shooting up his lower back with each powerful stride and concentrated on how good it felt to be back in the saddle.

Earlier, the stallion had made no attempt to bite or kick him when he threw the saddle on its back or fed the bit into its mouth, suggesting it too was glad to be free of the confines of the corral. Hoping that its good disposition would continue, Gabriel reined the horse in a little and the Morgan settled into a steady, mile-consuming lope.

The flat reddish scrubland, bathed in silver, fell behind them on both sides. In the distance thunderheads gathered above the peaks of the Organ Mountains. There was a strange quiet to the desert and Gabriel wondered if a storm was coming. Flash floods were common in the region and people trapped by them often drowned. He had to find Raven quickly.

He had no idea where she was. But remembering that she'd told him how Brandy had tried to ramrod her while they were hiding out in Furnace Canyon, he guided the horse in that direction.

Soon they reached the hills. He slowed the Morgan to a walk and followed the winding trail upward for about a mile before reaching the clumps of piñon trees and large craggy rocks that guarded the entrance to the box canyon.

As he rode into the canyon Gabriel

saw it was little more than a narrow, deep gash in the hills. Scraggly pines and shrubs clung to the steep sides. Ahead, the far end of the canyon was boxed in by a wall of rock. Gabriel gave the stallion its head. Brandy carefully picked its way along the trail, its hoofs clattering loudly over the loose stones. Along the ridgeline a pack of coyotes announced intruders were coming, their yip-yipping echoing off the canyon walls.

Gabriel knew that surprise was out of the question. He didn't care. He'd already figured out that he would never find Raven unless she wanted him to, so instead of wasting time tracking her he decided to lure her to him. Dismounting, he made a big fuss out of examining the Morgan's right hoof.

'Goddammit!' he said loudly. 'How the hell'd you cut yourself like that?' He looked back down the trail. 'Must've stepped on a sharp stone or somethin'. Of all the bad luck . . . ' Keeping hold of the reins, he sat on a rock and shook his head in disgust. 'Reckon all we can do now is sit here till daylight comes an' I can see exactly what's painin' you.'

As he spoke he listened carefully, trying to pick up any noise among the rocks surrounding him. Nothing stirred. If Raven was hiding within the sound of his voice, she was keeping still until she decided what to do.

Taking out the makings, Gabriel rolled a smoke and lit it. Then cupping his hands around the match, he again hunkered down and held the flame near the same rear leg. The match sputtered. Gabriel deliberately grabbed the leg and jerked it around. As he expected the stallion, tired of him messing with its leg, snorted and tried to cow-kick him.

Gabriel jumped back, avoiding the kick, yelling: 'Stand still, dammit — oww!' Pretending to be burned by the dying flame, he threw the match away and stood up. As he did he heard a faint giggle among the rocks to his left.

'That does it,' he told the horse. 'Come daylight, I'm leavin' you for coyote bait an' walkin' out of here.' He sat back on the rock and finished his smoke.

'You'd do it too, wouldn't you,' a small voice said. He looked up and saw Raven perched among the rocks.

'Damn right. An' don't go to frettin' about him either, 'cause he'd sure as hell'd do the same to me.'

'What do you expect,' she said, making her way down toward him, 'he's a horse. He doesn't know right from wrong. He just knows what he likes and doesn't like an' he doesn't like you.' She landed lightly on the ground beside Gabriel, moved close to the Morgan and began rubbing its velvety black nose.

The stallion nuzzled her, snickering softly. 'I'm sorry,' she told it. 'I don't have any piñon nuts. But I'll find you some on the way down.'

'Here,' Gabriel dug into the pocket of his jeans. 'Give him these.'

Raven saw the piñon nuts in the palm of his outstretched hand and looked at him as if he was giving away gold nuggets.

'What're you lookin' at?' Gabriel said wryly. 'You think I'm too old to learn?'

For another moment she continued to look at him and then she started giggling.

'What's so damn funny?'

'You,' she said. 'Thinking I'd fall for that dumb ol' horse-gone-lame trick.'

'If it's so dumb, why'd you show yourself?'

''Cause I got what I wanted.'

'What might that be?'

'You — to come after me.' Moving close, she hugged him. 'Now I know you care about me.'

He wanted to spank her. Instead, he held her away from him and looked sternly at her.

'I'm only here,' he lied, 'on account of your mother. How worried she was.'

'Fibber!' She jerked free and glared at him. 'If Momma was so worried why didn't she come an' look for me herself?'

'She wanted to. But I wouldn't let her.'

For a moment doubt showed in Raven's large black eyes. 'You're just saying that to make me feel bad.'

'Is it workin'?'

'Would you be happy if it was?'

'No. But, least I'd know you learned a lesson tonight.'

She gave him a confused, angry look. 'Why're you being so hateful?'

'Teachin' you to be responsible for your actions, that don't mean I hate you. Means I want you to grow up special.'

She wasn't buying it. 'Grown-ups,' she said bitterly. 'All you care about is preaching and punishing people.'

A coyote suddenly yipped high above them and at once his relatives all joined in, their yowling bouncing off the canyon walls.

Gabriel waited for the chorus to end before saying: 'If I was lookin' to punish you, girl, I would've put you 'cross my knee a minute ago.'

'You wouldn't dare!'

He lunged for her. But she was too quick. Grabbing the Morgan's mane, she swung up onto its back and dug her heels into its flanks.

'Git!' she yelled. The stallion launched itself into a gallop and disappeared into the dark box canyon.

Gabriel sighed, thinking as he did that he wasn't cut out to be a father. He then rolled another smoke and leaned back on the rock to enjoy it while he waited for her to return.

That Raven, he thought as he smoked. When she grows up, she's gonna be some kind of hellion.

14

The next morning broke cool and fresh. While Ingrid cooked breakfast, Gabriel and Raven hitched up the team and put all the valises in the back of the wagon. Earlier he had made a crude awning out of four poles and some canvas, attaching it over the wagon box so that mother and daughter would have cover from the broiling sun.

Raven was strangely silent as she worked alongside him. Gabriel guessed Ingrid must have laid down the law when he brought Raven home last night and other than saying good morning to her, kept to himself.

After breakfast, with the sun peeking over the eastern horizon, he saddled up the Morgan and waited by the wagon while Ingrid and Raven placed wild flowers on Sven's grave and then took a moment to say goodbye to the ranch.

Both were crying when they joined him.

'You probably think we're being overly sentimental,' Ingrid said to Gabriel as he helped her onto the wagon box.

'No, ma'am. Leavin' a beloved behind always hurts.'

'It's not just my husband,' Ingrid said wistfully. 'There are lots of wonderful memories here. Christmases, birthday parties, anniversaries . . . what good times we had.' She brushed a tear away before adding: 'Grandpa Johan and my father and grandfather built this place from the ground up. It was our wedding present. They planned on being finished the week before Sven and I got married. But wouldn't you know, it rained nonstop for two days, causing a flash flood, and most of the wood got washed away. Years later I remember Grandpa Johan laughing and saying how it took them hours to round it all up and bring it back here. Then they had to work like mad to get everything

117

done by our wedding day so we'd have a place to spend our honeymoon.'

'But they got it done,' Gabriel said. 'My book, that's what matters.'

Ingrid smiled at him. 'You are so like Sven.'

'I'll take that as a compliment.'

'I meant it as one.' She held his gaze for a moment then feeling herself blush, lowered her eyes.

Raven, who'd been watching them, saw her mother blush and felt a wave of jealousy. 'Bet you didn't know,' she said to Gabriel, 'that I was born here.'

'That right?'

'Exactly four minutes after two on a Sunday afternoon, right, Momma?'

'Yes, dear. Thank heavens it wasn't two in the morning or your father would never have been able to get the midwife over in time to help deliver you. My goodness,' she said, fondly brushing Raven's hair back from her face, 'you were such a beautiful baby.'

'I was?'

'Had the biggest, darkest, prettiest

118

eyes anyone ever saw. And still do.'

Raven, as if overwhelmed by the thought, suddenly put her arms around Ingrid. 'I love you, Momma.'

'Love you too, lamb.' They hugged for another moment then Ingrid picked up the reins and snapped them, setting the team in motion.

Gabriel pulled his old campaign hat over his eyes to keep out the sun then nudged the Morgan into a walk and the three of them set off for Las Cruces.

The most direct route was an old Butterfield Stagecoach trail that had been abandoned once the railroad arrived. To get to it they had to cross five miles of open desert dotted with dry brush and chaparral. The terrain never varied. By mid morning the sun had climbed high into the naked sky and the heat was remorseless. Now and then they stopped to rest the horses and to take a sip of water. But for the most part they trudged along, eating dust, seldom saying a word.

Finally, Gabriel found the winding,

rutted stagecoach trail and signaled for Ingrid to park the wagon in a tiny patch of shade beside a rocky outcrop.

'Now'd be a good time to stretch your legs,' he advised, dismounting. 'We got a long ride ahead of us and for the most part there ain't much cover.'

Welcoming the rest, Ingrid let Gabriel help her down from the wagon. When he turned to help Raven, she refused his hand and jumped off on her own. Amused, Gabriel joined Ingrid who had plopped down on a flat rock. Loosening the front of her shirt, she began fanning herself with her hand.

'My God, it's scorching.'

Gabriel rolled and lit a smoke and then fanned her with his hat.

'Oh, that's wonderful.' She closed her eyes, leaned back and enjoyed the cool air. 'Days like this I wish I'd never left home.'

'It doesn't get hot in Norway, ma'am?'

'Not like this, never. It can get quite warm in summer. But summer only lasts from the end of June to early August, and for the most part it's very pleasant.'

'I once read how the sun shines at midnight. 'Course I knew that couldn't be true, but — '

'Oh, but it is. North of the Arctic Circle the sun's so close to the horizon that it shines all day and night during the summer months. That's why we call it the Midnight Sun.'

'How 'bout that?' Gabriel said, impressed. 'Learn somethin' every day.'

Raven, irked by the attention he was paying her mother, went to the water barrel Gabriel had lashed to the side of the wagon. Filling a bowl, she gave the two team horses a drink.

'Not too much,' Gabriel warned. 'Don't want 'em to bloat up in this heat.' She gave him a withering look as if to say she already knew that, and then refilled the bowl and held it under the Morgan's muzzle.

'Would you like a ham sandwich?'

Ingrid asked her. 'I made some before we left in case we got hungry.'

'No.'

'No, what?'

'Thank you.' Pouting, Raven sat beside the Morgan and released her hostility by hurling stones at a road-runner that was crossing the trail. The black-and-white mottled bird with its distinctive head crest and upward tail dodged them easily and fled in a blur.

Ingrid sighed and shook her head. 'I hope she's not going to be like this the whole way or it's going to be a very long trip.'

'She'll perk up soon as you get on the train,' Gabriel said. 'Be a new experience for her. She won't have time to sulk.'

'Speaking of trains, what do you plan to do once we get to Las Cruces? After you've seen Ellen, I mean?'

'Haven't given it much thought.'

'Can you stay in town if you want to?'

'Mean am I wanted by the law there?

Yep. Stadtlander made sure of that. New Mexico, Arizona, Texas — man as rich an' powerful as him has got a mighty long reach.'

'Then you mustn't go there. Once we get close to town you must ride off. Surely you can see that?'

'You're forgettin' Ellie, ma'am. Promised myself I'd see her. 'Sides, the mission's 'bout two miles away in Mesilla. So long as I don't cause trouble chances are the sheriff won't come after me. Not for his wages.'

Ingrid hesitated. She wanted to ask him to come to California with them, but couldn't find the nerve. 'Well, I think you're making a dreadful mistake. I'm sure Ellie would too. But of course you won't listen to me. So whatever you do I wish you luck.'

'You, too. Maybe one day we'll meet up again.'

'I'd like that. And I know Raven would, too.'

Neither seemed to know what to say next and there was an awkward pause.

'Reckon we better be movin'.' Rising, Gabriel stubbed his cigarette out on the heel of his boot, hitched up his gun-belt so it rested on his hips and walked to the Morgan. About to step into the saddle, he faked a lunge at Raven as if to grab her. But she sprang back, avoiding him.

'Hah! You can't catch me. I'm too quick for you.'

He turned his back on her, as if the game was over. Raven fell for it and walked to the wagon. A faint whirring sound made her turn — but she was too late. His rope looped around her. She tried to wriggle free but Gabriel jerked the noose tight, clamping her arms to her sides, and then slowly, hand over hand, pulled her to him.

Ingrid, watching from the wagon, began laughing.

Gabriel pulled Raven right up to him then held the rope up just high enough to bring her to her toes.

'Now what was that you were sayin'?' he asked her.

'Let-me-go,' she hissed at him. 'Momma, tell him to let me go!'

Gabriel grinned at Ingrid. 'How 'bout I put her 'cross my knee and give her a few licks?'

'Hmmm,' she said impishly. 'Not a bad idea.'

'Momma, you make him let me go this instant or I'll never speak to you again.'

Ingrid cupped a hand to her ear. 'Did you hear something, Mr Moonlight? Or was that just the wind?'

'Momma!'

'The wind, ma'am, I reckon.'

'MOMMA!'

Ingrid chuckled. 'What do you say, Mr Moonlight? Do we give her one more chance?'

'Seems reasonable.' He let the rope go slack, loosening the loop around Raven. Immediately she squirmed out of it and ran off, stopping only when she was out of his reach.

She glared at them. 'You'll be sorry. Both of you!' Before either of them could stop her, she swung up onto the stallion and galloped off.

'Raven — come back here!'

'Let her go,' Gabriel said. 'If there was ever two of a kind deserved each other, they're it.'

She was waiting for them about a half mile up the trail. As the wagon approached, she got up from the rock on which she'd been resting and offered the reins to Gabriel.

'Keep ridin',' he told her. He indicated the awning overhead. 'It's a mite cooler where I'm sittin'.'

Exasperated, Raven mounted up and fell in beside the wagon.

★ ★ ★

They reached Munsey's Trading Post around noon. Knowing there was another six hours of hard traveling ahead of them, Gabriel suggested they give themselves and the horses a much-needed rest.

There were three, sweat-lathered

saddled ponies hitched to the rail outside the large, adobe-walled building and two other wagons had just pulled out. Gabrielle watched them plodding toward the horizon for a moment then unhitched the team and led them to the drinking trough. Raven had already taken the Morgan there and, as Gabriel approached, the all-black stallion lifted its dripping muzzle from the water and snorted, warning him to stay clear. Gabriel ignored Brandy and told Raven to join her mother, who was looking for something in one of the valises.

'Tell her yourself. You're not my father.'

'Don't try to buffalo me,' he warned gently. 'I'm hot an' tired an' leanin' toward irritable. So go round up your mom an' the two of you go on inside an' get washed up. By then I'll be ready to join you. Mrs Munsey sets a fine table.'

'Mean we're gonna eat here?'

'My treat.'

'But what about the sandwiches?'

'We'll save 'em for later. Nothin' but desert 'tween here an' Las Cruces — ' He broke off as two disheveled-looking men with beards and long straggly hair came out of the trading post. One glimpse told Gabriel they were saddle tramps. They wore long grimy dusters over their soiled clothing, pants tucked into knee-high boots, and sweat-stained hats that hung down their backs, Mexican-style. They staggered drunkenly as they walked, and the larger man held a near-empty bottle of whiskey in his fist.

They stopped as they saw Ingrid, grinned at each other and lurched toward her.

'Stay here,' Gabriel told Raven. He started for the wagon, unhurried but purposeful, his gun hand hanging loosely beside his holster.

Neither man saw him coming; they were too focused on Ingrid. She, in turn, didn't see them. Bent over the open valise, engrossed in her search, they were on her before she knew it.

'Well, lookee here, Jesse,' the big man said. 'We found us a woman.'

'Yeah,' said Jesse. He stroked Ingrid's hair. 'If y'ain't the purtiest damn filly I ever did see.'

Alarmed, she tried to squeeze past them. But they grabbed her and pinned her back against the wagon.

'P-please,' she begged, 'let me go.'

'Sure, sure, all in good time . . . ' Jesse ripped open her shirt and clumsily fondled her breasts.

Ingrid jerked away. 'Stoppit! Don't you dare touch me!'

'Hear that, Turk?' Jesse grinned at his partner. 'Little lady here don't want me to touch her.'

'Teach her a lesson, Jesse. G'wan. Show her who's ramrod.'

Jesse laughed, showing broken snuff-stained teeth, and tried to kiss Ingrid. She twisted her face away. He grabbed her by the chin, forced her to face him and again tried to kiss her. She bit his lip, bringing blood. Cursing, he went to slap her.

Ingrid cringed, but to her surprise the blow never came. Hit from behind by Gabriel's Colt, Jesse's eyes suddenly rolled up into his head and he crumpled to the ground.

Turk gaped at Gabriel, who now leveled his gun at him.

'D-don't shoot, mister,' he stammered, hands raised. 'Please. We didn't mean no harm. We was jes' funnin' with her. I swear . . . '

Gabriel, eyes ablaze, thumbed back the hammer.

'Leather it!' a voice snarled behind him.

Gabriel looked over his shoulder. A third saddle tramp, who'd just stepped out of the trading post, moved toward him. He looked and smelled as badly as the others. Difference was he was aiming a scattergun at Gabriel and Ingrid.

'Y'heard me, mister. Do like I say or you an' the skirt get blown to yesterday.'

Gabriel slowly slid his Colt back into the holster.

'That's more like it,' said the man

with the shotgun. 'You awright, Turk?'

'Be a helluva lot better when I shoot this no-good sonofabitch!'

'What's left of him, y'mean.' He began to squeeze the trigger — when a small stone struck him on the temple, stunning him.

Even as the man crumpled to the ground Gabriel drew his Colt, fired and put a bullet between Turk's eyes. Turk collapsed, gun still in his holster.

Ingrid turned away, sickened.

Gabriel whirled and aimed his gun at Jesse, who still lay in the dirt but was starting to come around.

'Go on,' Raven urged. 'What're you waiting for? Kill him. If you don't,' she added when he didn't move, 'I will.' Putting another stone in her slingshot, she angrily pulled it back and aimed at Jesse's head.

'No!' Ingrid stepped between Jesse and her daughter. 'For God's sake, child, put that thing away! Hasn't there been enough killing!'

'But, Momma, they were gonna hurt

131

you. They ain't fit to live.'

'Do like she says,' Gabriel said quietly. Holstering his Colt, he helped Ingrid to her feet. He then looked at Jesse, who was bleeding from a swollen cut on his temple. 'Ride,' he said grimly, 'an' take that scum-eatin' filth with you.'

Rising, Jesse dragged his dead partners to their horses, threw them over their saddles, grabbed the reins and rode off.

'We're done here,' Gabriel told Ingrid. He helped her onto the wagon box. Then he put his arm around Raven's shoulders and said so only she could hear: 'Look after your mom while I get the horses. She needs you.'

'Me?'

'Sure. Don't always take a lifetime, y'know.'

'What doesn't?'

'Bein' responsible.'

'What?'

'Sometimes, just like now, person gets all growed up in seconds.' Patting her on the head, he walked toward the team.

'Aren't you even gonna thank me?'

'I just did,' Gabriel said. 'Think about it.'

15

It was dark when they reached the outskirts of Las Cruces.

Once a dusty little Mexican village located at the foot of the Organ Mountains, it had acquired its name in 1830 when a group of travelers were massacred by Apaches and crosses were put on their graves. Then in 1882 the arrival of the Santa Fe Railroad transformed it into a bustling town with a courthouse, six hotels and almost twenty saloons. There was also a sheriff's office and jail, numerous stores and churches, schools and a residential area where large hip-roofed houses on grassy lawns dwarfed the rows of traditional one-story adobe homes.

At the edge of town, bordering the desert, there stood a large walled compound known as Ft. Seldon. Manned by black troopers whom the Indians called Buffalo Soldiers, it had been built to protect the settlers from marauding Apaches; but with Geronimo's capture it had outlasted its usefulness and was now due to be closed.

Gabriel, astride the Morgan, led the wagon past the fort on into town. They cut through the Mexican section, riding past cantinas, adobe hovels and a mariachi band playing in a small dirt plaza, and finally reached Main Street. Though it was supper time the sidewalks were crowded and buckboards and wagons were everywhere. Gabriel kept his eye out for the law as he rode alongside the wagon. None of the townspeople paid attention to them but Ingrid, concerned for his safety, begged him to ride straight to the mission. He stubbornly refused, and insisted on making sure they were comfortably ensconced in the Hickory Hotel before leaving them.

'I'll be back in the mornin' to take you to the train,' he told Ingrid.

Worried about his safety yet wanting

to see him one more time, she said only: 'If you insist.'

Gabriel fondly tousled Raven's hair, 'Right proud of you, scout,' and was gone before she could answer.

* * *

There was a livery stable on the next corner. Gabriel turned the Morgan and team over to the old bearded hostler, paid him for one night's keep, along with a dollar tip, and thumbed at the hay loft above them. 'Mind if I stretch out for a few hours?'

The hostler leaned on his hay fork, sized Gabriel up, and spat tobacco juice into a pile of hay. 'For one more of these,' he said, holding up the silver dollar, 'you can keep the mice company all night.'

Gabriel handed him the dollar, hefted his saddle onto his shoulder and climbed the ladder up to the loft.

'Might you be expectin' any visitors, son?'

'Just the mayor an' a ten-piece brass band,' Gabriel said.

'Figgered as much.' The hostler chuckled, spat again and continued forking hay into the feed boxes.

★   ★   ★

Dawn was still an hour away when Gabriel swung into the saddle and nudged the Morgan out of the livery stable. The mission convent was only two miles away in Mesilla, but he wanted to get there early so he didn't have to rush his visit with Ellie and still be back in time to take Ingrid and Raven to the station.

Taking care of them had become important to him. He didn't know exactly when it had started but he now knew Ingrid meant something to him and he felt fatherly toward Raven. Vexing and rebellious as she was, he knew that if he'd been lucky enough to live a normal life and raise a daughter he would have wanted her to be like

Raven. As for Ingrid, a man would be hard-pressed to find a better woman. Too bad, he thought, that fate had chosen another trail for him . . .

The town was quiet. Still. Gabriel felt a cold wind off the desert chilling his face as he rode toward the outskirts. He kept to the unlighted side streets, hoping to avoid running into a patrolling lawman, the steady thud-thudding of the stallion's hoofs on the dirt a lulling rhythm in his ears.

As he rode he tried to imagine how surprised Ellie would be when she saw him. His last memory of her was an ugly one. Knowing he'd been shot, she begged him to let her take him to the doctor in Santa Rosa. He refused, assuring her that his wound wasn't severe. By her expression he knew he hadn't fooled her, but she was wise enough to realize he didn't want her to see him die and let the matter drop. She just sat there, astride the leggy blue roan, tears running down her lovely face. At death's door, he'd then kissed her hand and promised to write her soon as he reached California, believing even as he spoke that he'd never see her again.

Well, he thought now, he hadn't lied to her after all. Because in a few minutes he'd be able to hold her again; and though her love would never belong to anyone but God, at least from now on they would occasionally get to see one another.

The thought of that made him smile.

★　★　★

Leaving Las Cruces, Gabriel rode south and soon entered the outskirts of Mesilla. As he looked about him he realized nothing had changed since his last visit.

Before he'd holed up in Mexico he'd often met Cally in one of the many backstreet cantinas, knowing that if he didn't cause any trouble the law, such as it was, wouldn't bother him. And here he was, he realized, five years later riding in to meet her sister.

At a convent!

Fate was sure strange.

But then the history of the little village, he knew, was equally strange. During the Civil War Mesilla had served as the capital of the Confederate Territory of Arizona; later it became known as the 'hub' of the entire region and the crossroads for two important stagecoach lines, Butterfield and the Santa Fe Trail. At the time, adjoining it was a smaller, sleepier village known as Las Cruces. Neither was expected to ever grow into a city. But of the two Mesilla, she of the bawdy cantinas and festivals that were frequented by Billy the Kid, Jessie Evans and Pat Garrett, would have been the choice if anyone asked.

Then in 1881 the Santa Fe Railroad offered to pay the citizens of Mesilla for the right to build a railroad through town. The people agreed but the price they demanded for the land was too high. The railroad men looked elsewhere.

They discovered neighboring Las Cruces wasn't so greedy. Visionaries, the towns-people knew their future lay with the railroad and offered their land for free. The rest was history.

Ahead, Gabriel saw the old adobe church and buildings of the Sisters of Mercy convent silhouetted in the dawn light. Reining up, he dismounted, tied the Morgan to a tree and approached the chapel-shaped wooden gate. It opened at his touch. Removing his hat, he walked up the flagstone path to the front door. Lights showed in some of the windows. The nuns, as he had expected, were early risers. Hoping he wasn't disturbing their prayers, he took a deep breath to settle his nerves and pulled the bell-rope.

Shortly the door opened and an elderly nun in a black habit and a medieval white coronet smiled serenely at him. 'Yes? May I help you?'

'I'm here to see someone, sister.'

Her gray eyes looked at the gun on his hip then lifted to meet his gaze and held steadily. 'Are you sure you have the right place?'

'Yes, ma'am.'

'I see. Then perhaps you'd better tell me her name.'

'Kincaide, sister. Ellen Kincaide.'

'Ahh,' the old nun frowned. 'Dear me, I hope you haven't traveled too far.'

'Far enough. Why?'

'I'm afraid Sister Kincaide has left us.'

Gabriel's heart sank. 'She's passed on, you mean?'

'Oh, no. Sister Kincaide's in excellent health. But she decided to serve the Lord at another mission.'

'An' where might that be, sister?'

The old nun hesitated and he could tell she was trying to decide if she should reveal Ellen's whereabouts to a stranger.

'It's mighty important,' he said. 'Ellie thinks I'm dead and I want her to know I ain't.'

'Oh, my gracious . . . yes . . . yes, I can see where that would be important.

Well,' the old nun said cautiously, 'I can't tell you exactly where Sister Kincaide went — she wasn't sure herself when she left. But I can tell you that her intended destination was California — Carmel, I believe she said.' She paused and reflected sadly for a moment. 'We all thought she was making a mistake. Mother Superior tried hard to change her mind but Sister Kincaide couldn't be swayed. Said her destiny awaited her there and off she went.'

'Caught the train, did she?'

'Yes. Week or so ago. I'm sorry you missed her,' she said, seeing Gabriel's disappointment. 'I'm sure Sister Kincaide would have enjoyed seeing you. She hasn't been her usual cheerful self of late and I think now I understand why.'

Thanking her, Gabriel dug some money from his pocket and stuffed it into the nun's aged hands. 'Put this to good use.'

'God speed,' she said gratefully and crossed herself.

16

As he rode away from Mesilla a storm thundered over the Organ Mountains. A sudden stray shower soaked Gabriel. But the rain only lasted briefly and by the time he'd reached Las Cruces, stopped in at the livery stable and hitched the team to the wagon the sun was shining again and he soon dried off.

Ingrid and Raven were waiting in the hotel lobby when Gabriel drove up. Raven, who'd been watching through the window, ran out to greet him.

'Can I ride Brandy to the station?' she begged as he climbed down. 'Can I, Gabe? Can I? Please?'

'Sure. But stay close, scout. If someone recognizes me, we'll need to trade places pronto.'

As he was untying the Morgan from the wagon, it tried to bite him. Cursing, he slapped it with his hat.

Raven scowled at him. 'You're never gonna get to be his friend like that.'

'I don't want to be his friend,' Gabriel said. 'Hell, only reason I'm keepin' him around is so when he gets old I can sell him for dog food.'

'Don't listen to him,' she whispered to the stallion. 'He's an old meany. Besides, I'd steal you away from him 'fore I'd let him do something like that.'

Behind them, Ingrid emerged from the hotel followed by a bellhop with their valises. Gabriel tipped him, threw the bags in the wagon and helped her onto the seat.

'Sleep well, ma'am?'

'Very well, thank you.'

'Fibber,' Raven said. 'Momma was worried about you,' she told Gabriel. 'Hardly slept a wink.'

'Raven — '

'Kept talkin' in her sleep, too. Should've heard all the things she said.'

'Enough!' Ingrid rolled her eyes at Gabriel. 'I swear she has no sense of decency whatsoever.'

Gabriel grinned, snapped the reins and the wagon lurched forward.

They rode along Main Street in the direction of the train station. Towns-people occasionally glanced their way. But no one recognized Gabriel and they went on about their business.

'How was Ellen?' Ingrid asked Gabriel. 'Overjoyed to see you, no doubt?'

'Ellie wasn't there. 'Cording to one of the sisters, she left a few days ago for another mission.'

'Oh, that's too bad.' Though sad for him Ingrid felt a glow of relief. 'So will you be going there next?'

'I'm considerin' it.'

'Is the mission far away?' Raven asked.

'Far enough,' Gabriel said. He fell silent and Ingrid shook her head at Raven, warning her not to bother him again.

Shortly, they turned down Depot Street, a narrow road that led to the train station. The railroad had paved it

146

when they laid the tracks and then gone on to build a fine station-house — three large wood-frame buildings with slanted roofs that shaded passengers waiting on the platform.

Parking the wagon by the entrance, Gabriel unloaded the valises while Ingrid and Raven entered the station-house to buy tickets to Sacramento. From there, according to Reece's last letter, they could catch a Southern Pacific branch line to Old Calico. 'I only mention this, sis,' he'd written, 'in case something unforeseen happens & I can't meet you or send one of my men to meet you.' He'd ended the letter by saying: 'I'm looking forward to seeing you again, Ingrid, & of course Raven, whom I've seen so seldom. Have a safe & comfortable journey. Respectfully yours, your loving brother, Reece.'

Gabriel carried the bags to a shady bench on the platform and waited for Ingrid and Raven to join him. With Ellen gone and a posse hunting him, he realized he had no reason to stay in

147

New Mexico or any of the other states in which he was wanted. California, on the other hand, looked mighty appealing. He would be close to the three people who meant most to him and finally free of the stigma: 'horse-thief.'

Or would he, he wondered. Stadtlander was a vindictive man capable of cruel, ruthless reprisals. In the years Gabriel had worked for him he'd seen how Stadtlander held grudges against people for the slightest offense. And Gabriel's offense wasn't slight: he had killed the rancher's son, Slade, his only remaining flesh and blood, and he doubted if Stadtlander would ever forgive him. More likely he'd use his wealth and influence to track Gabriel down wherever he went. And once he found him, he'd stop at nothing to kill him. Pinkerton agents, bounty hunters, legitimate lawmen — all would be hunting Gabriel for the big reward Stadtlander was bound to offer.

No, Gabriel thought bitterly, there was only one way to end this continuing vendetta and that was to kill Stadt-lander —

'Train's due in ten minutes!' Raven's excited voice interrupted his thoughts.

He turned as she came running up to him. 'Sounds like you can't wait to get rid of me.'

'Quicker the better,' she quipped. 'I don't mean that,' she added quickly. 'I'm gonna miss you. Lots.'

'Me, too.' He curled his arm around her slender waist and pulled her down on his lap. She made no attempt to break loose. And when he looked into her big black eyes he saw tears welling into them.

'Be sure'n take good care of your mother, y'hear?'

'Yes, sir.'

'An' write me.'

'How will I know where you are?'

'Because he's going to write to me,' Ingrid said, joining them. She handed Gabriel a slip of paper bearing her brother's address. 'And in that letter he's going to tell us where he is and how he's doing, isn't that right, Gabe?'

'Yep. So you see,' he told Raven, 'you got no excuse for not writin'. Now, give me a big hug, scout, an' then let me have a minute alone with your mom.'

Raven hugged him, her tears wetting his cheek. 'I love you,' she whispered. 'And I will write. You'll see. You just better write back!'

He squeezed her, feeling emotions he'd never thought existed in him and then released her. He felt her spring away from him and watched as she ran off down the platform.

'It's not too late to change your mind,' Ingrid said. 'The stationmaster said the train isn't full. And you know how much we'd love to have you come along.'

'Maybe one day,' Gabriel said.

She sensed he was evading her question and saw a glint in his eyes that frightened her.

'Oh, my God,' she exclaimed. 'You're thinking of killing Stillman Stadtlander, aren't you?'

He wanted to say no but he couldn't lie to her.

His silence confirmed she was right. She knew then she'd lost him and she felt cold and empty inside.

'Men,' she said angrily. 'You make me so mad. You're willing to throw away everything just to fight windmills.'

'This particular windmill's tryin' to kill me an' he won't stop till one of us is dead.'

'All the more reason for you to come to California.'

'Like I told you once before — runnin' ain't the answer.'

'Getting killed to prove a point is?'

'I don't aim on gettin' killed. But if it's in the cards, then so be it. I know how to die standin' up, Ingrid.'

It was the first time he'd called her by name and the fact that he'd waited until now, when it was too late to matter, only made her angrier.

'Oh yes. I'd forgotten. The code! Your precious code!' Tears of pent-up rage and frustration now ran down her cheeks. 'Well, Mr Gabriel Moonlight, let me tell what I think of your code. I think it's just an excuse men made up so they can ride around slaying dragons, dragons that could easily be ignored but have to be killed so men can feel noble and brave even if it costs them their lives and hurts everyone around them — '

He kissed her, cutting off her angry tirade. Surprised, she responded with more passion than he'd expected. Then both of them heard a distant train whistle and felt the ground trembling and knew it was over.

'I'm goin' now,' Gabriel said, releasing her. He stood up, towering over her, surprised by how much the kiss had affected him. 'When I get back to town I'll sell your wagon an' team an' send you the money.'

'Keep it,' Ingrid said, fighting not to cry. 'It'll pay for your ticket should you ever feel like coming to see me.'

She watched him walk away, tall and wide-shouldered, his long-legged strides soon carrying him to the end of the platform and on around the station-house, out of sight.

'Momma, Momma, the train's coming!'

'I know, lamb. I hear it.' Ingrid wiped her tears away and turned to her daughter. 'Can you believe it? We're on our way to California.'

Raven nodded and turned to face the oncoming train, trying as she did not to think about how much she would miss Gabriel.

17

The hostler was sweeping out the livery stable when Gabriel drove up in the wagon. The old gray-bearded man leaned on his broom and stared at the gunfighter in surprise.

'Didn't 'spect to see you again, son.'

'Forgot to say *adios* to the mice.'

The hostler chuckled and spat at a spider scurrying for cover, drenching it in tobacco juice. 'What can I do for you?'

'Lookin' to sell this rig. Know anyone who might be interested?'

'Mebbe.' The old man walked slowly around the wagon and horses, sizing them up. 'How much y'askin'?'

'Make an offer.'

'Gotta talk to a fella first.'

Guessing the hostler had a buyer in mind Gabriel untied the Morgan from the rear of the wagon, stepped into the saddle and thumbed at the cantina across the street. 'When you're ready, old timer, I'll be in there. But keep in mind the money's for a widow with a young'un, so make your offer fair.' He nudged the Morgan in the direction of the cantina.

★　★　★

Two tequilas chased by a beer and a plate of tortillas and beans later, Gabriel saw the hostler push in through the swing-doors. Pausing long enough to let his eyes grow accustomed to the dimness, he came bustling over to Gabriel's table.

'Don't know if it's fair or not,' he said, placing a wad of bills before Gabriel, 'but two hundred's all I could rustle up.'

'Horses alone are worth that, if not more.'

'Take it or leave it, Mr Jennings.'

Gabriel instinctively dropped his hand to his gun.

'Got no call to shoot me, son. I coulda kept the money an' the rig if I'd felt inclined. But you been square with me, so — '

'Get to the meat, old timer.'

'Sheriff's got his deputies combin' the town for you.'

'You tell 'em I was here?'

'If I was younger, sonny, I'd take offense to that.'

Gabriel sighed wearily, stuffed the money into his pocket and got to his feet.

'They headed this way?'

'Only a matter of time. Soon as Sheriff Akins told his men ol' man Stadtlander had upped the price on your head, they set off like a pack of hungry dogs.'

Gabriel felt a surge of anger. 'Is he here — Stadtlander, I mean?'

'Sheriff's office, last I heard.'

'How many guns with him?'

'Six or seven. But you won't have to deal with 'em. They're out helpin' the deputies hunt you.'

Gabriel offered his hand to the hostler. ''Bliged.'

'You'da done the same,' the old man said. 'Now git.'

★ ★ ★

Keeping to the backstreets Gabriel rode toward the sheriff's office. As if sensing the urgency of his mission, the normally irascible Morgan made no attempt to be skittish or buck him off; and though Gabriel still didn't trust it, the horse remained docile and obedient, following every command Gabriel gave it.

Sun beating down on them, they cut through the Mexican section of town. Dirt streets, adobe hovels, fruit stands, leather shops, children with outstretched hands clamoring for him to stop — all reminded Gabriel of his years of exile south of the border. It also increased his determination to end Stadtlander's hold over him.

They entered a sun-bleached alley striped with shadows. Barely wide enough for two horsemen to pass, it led between the backs of several buildings to the rear of the jail adjoining the sheriff's office. Two saddled horses stood tied to a hitching rail.

Gabriel dismounted, looped the reins over the rail and pulled his Winchester from the saddle boot. Pumping a shell into the chamber, he followed the blank wall of the jail to the end and then ducked into another, narrower alley that ended at Main Street. Keeping close to the wall Gabriel peered out and saw wagons, buckboards and riders passing by, townspeople going about their business, and two old timers jawing outside the sheriff's office. He waited impatiently for them to stop arguing and stomp off in opposite directions and then walked casually along the sidewalk to the front door. It opened at his touch and he ducked inside, finger on the trigger, ready to shoot anyone who opposed him.

The office was empty. He moved quietly to an inner door that he guessed led back to the jail. Pushing it open with his rifle, he peered inside — and saw a young, one-legged jailor dozing in a hard-backed chair. Gabriel poked him with his Winchester. The man came awake instantly and froze as he saw the rifle and who was holding it.

'Easy,' Gabriel warned. 'Tell me where Mr Stadtlander is an' you can go back to sleep.'

'With the sheriff. 'Cross the street havin' a drink.'

'Place got a name?'

'Garrett's.'

Gabriel nodded and tapped his rifle butt against the jailor's head, knocking him senseless. Taking his keys, Gabriel re-entered the office, locked the door, threw the keys under the desk and walked out.

No one paid attention to him as he crossed the busy street to Garrett's, a small wood-fronted building with traditional bat-wing doors named after the sheriff who'd killed Billy the Kid. Ducking into an alley beside the saloon

Gabriel entered through a back door. To his left was a storeroom, to his right a kitchen and directly ahead a door leading into the bar. Gabriel inched it open and peered through the crack.

A bartender was pouring whiskey for three cowboys at the bar. Behind him, above the cash register and a display of liquor, hung a gilt-edged mirror in which Gabriel could see the reflection of Sheriff Samuel Akins and Stillman Stadtlander.

The two men were talking at a corner table, a bottle of rye before them. Gabriel made sure no one else was in the bar then pushed open the door and covered Stadtlander and the burly, mustachioed lawman with his rifle.

Everyone but Stadtlander froze. The tough old rancher, shoulders hunched over from arthritis, chuckled as if seeing an old friend and shook his head in admiration.

'I was expectin' you to make a play, Gabe. Barkeep, another glass.'

'Save it,' Gabriel waved off the

160

bartender. 'Won't be here long enough for a drink.'

'Don't be a damn fool,' Sheriff Akins told him. He was a big man, full of self-importance, but he had a woman's voice. 'Y'ain't goin' nowhere. You so much as step outside an' my men'll cut you to pieces.'

'I just come from outside, sheriff. Not a deputy in sight. You,' Gabriel wagged his Winchester at the bartender who was reaching for something. 'Bring your hands up real slow and don't let me see anythin' in 'em.' Then as the bartender slowly obeyed: 'Come out from behind there.'

He waited until the bartender was in front of the bar then turned back to Stadtlander and the sheriff.

'So what happens next?' the rancher asked him.

Gabriel set the rifle on the table next to him and let his gun-hand drop beside his holster.

'I was hopin' we could end our differences right here an' now.'

Stadtlander grinned mirthlessly. 'I'd like to oblige you, son, but it seems the Good Lord has other plans.' He raised his gun-hand and Gabriel saw arthritis had turned it into a half-closed claw. 'Throw in my broken ribs, gimpy leg an' bad back an' you'd get more fight from a blind gandy dancer.'

As he finished speaking one of the cowboys at the bar moved slightly. That movement, twitch, saved Gabriel's life. His eyes flicked in the cowboy's direction — and in that instant he saw in the mirror the reflection of Stadtlander's other hand reaching under the table and drawing a derringer from his boot.

He drew his Colt and fired, so quickly the bullet knocked Stadtlander from his chair before the derringer cleared the table.

Sheriff Samuel Akins threw up his hands and blurted: 'I ain't drawin' against you, Moonlight. Y'all can see that.'

Gabriel ignored him. Stepping close

to Stadtlander, he kicked the derringer aside and looked down at him.

Stadtlander lay on his back, blood seeping from his shoulder, teeth gritted against the pain. 'W-why didn't you kill me?' he said bitterly. 'Can't you see I got nothin' to live for?'

'Windmills,' Gabriel said, holstering his Colt. 'I'm all through fightin' 'em.' Picking up his Winchester he prodded the sheriff with it, forcing him to stand up. 'Let's go.'

'Where?'

'Pick up our horses.'

Stadtlander raised up on one elbow. 'You arrogant pup! You really think you can just ride out of here?'

'That depends on Sam, here.' Gabriel turned to Sheriff Akins. 'When we get outside, I see any of your deputies or Stadtlander's men pointin' a gun at me, I'll put a bullet in your spine. May not kill you right away but you'll surely wish it had.'

163

18

Raven was depressed.

A sudden thunderstorm over the Cookes Range, followed by torrential rain, had turned the local creeks and gullies into dangerous, fast-moving rivers. A flash flood had also washed out the railroad tracks twelve miles east of Deming, forcing the train on which she and her mother were traveling to stop.

Hunched down in her seat in the passenger car, she sat with her nose pressed against the window, glumly watching the rain lashing against the glass and wondering how long they would be stuck here.

Two hours earlier she had asked the conductor the same question. He hadn't been much help. He'd telegraphed the stationmaster at Deming he said, and workmen were on their way, but in this kind of weather who knew how long it would take them to get here. Hours, days, maybe even weeks. He winked at Ingrid to let her know he was joking, and then continued on.

One of the four well-dressed, silver-haired men playing poker across the aisle turned to Raven and remarked that she should consider herself lucky.

She could tell he was being condescending and disliked him immediately. 'Oh? Why's that?'

'Be polite now,' her mother whispered.

'Back in the '70s, little gal,' the man said pompously, ''fore the Iron Horse replaced Mr Butterfield's stage line an' that hellion Geronimo was runnin' wild, you would've been more concerned 'bout keepin' your pretty hair than a little rain storm.'

'No, I wouldn't,' she said. 'Geronimo wouldn't have bothered me. Go ahead an' laugh,' she said as the man and the other players chuckled, 'it's true. My grandpa saved the life of Almighty Sky, medicine man of all the Mescaleros, and from then on the Apaches were our friends.'

The story sounded preposterous, but Raven spoke with such sincerity it was hard not to believe her. The four poker players exchanged questioning looks. Then the pompous man tapped the ash from his cigar and turned to Ingrid, who was quietly crocheting, and inquired: 'Is that true, ma'am?'

'Sure is,' a voice said behind them.

Everyone turned and looked at the tall, rain-soaked man standing by the door. He'd just entered and water from the brim of his old campaign hat and yellow slicker was pooling around his boots.

'I can vouch for it. Apaches saved my life an' it was all on 'count of her an' her mom.'

The pompous man cleared his throat. 'I'm very sorry, little gal,' he began. 'I didn't mean to insinuate — '

He got no further. Raven, who like her mother had been staring at the

166

stranger in shock, now jumped up and ran to him.

'G-Gabe!' she flung herself into his arms and burst into tears. 'W-what're you doing — I mean, h-how did you get here? I never thought I'd see y-you again!'

'Had some doubts 'bout that myself,' he said, thinking about how hard he'd ridden the Morgan. 'But thanks to the delay an' a shortcut through Massacre Pass I was able to catch up with you.'

'Mean you're comin' with us?'

'Far as Sacramento, yeah.' Scooping Raven up in his arms, he carried her to her seat and stood in the aisle smiling down at Ingrid. 'If that still meets with your approval?'

'I don't know,' she said, playing along.

'Momma!'

Ignoring Raven's angry protest, she added:

'I'll have to think about it.'

'Sounds reasonable.' Gabriel set Raven down and wiped the rain from his eyes. 'Now if you ladies will excuse me, I'll go make sure Brandy doesn't kick nobody while they're loadin' him on the train.' With a polite tip of his hat, he turned, opened the door and stepped out into the rain.

19

California

It was mid morning when the train carrying Gabriel, Ingrid and Raven finally pulled into the Central Pacific Railroad depot alongside the Sacramento River.

At that hour the stationhouse, freight yard and bustling waterfront were at their busiest. Mule-drawn wagons were lined up twenty deep as the drivers waited their turn to unload their cargo onto the decks of the paddle-wheel steamers tied up along the riverbank. Wranglers shouted and cracked their long whips as they herded sheep and cattle up ramps leaned against the vessels. The bleating and bellowing of the animals, mingled with the clanging of streetcars and whistles from arriving and departing steamers was deafening.

Opposite the station was a shack with a rooftop sign that advertised: 'California Steam Navigation Company — Steamers for San Francisco. Cabin $5 — Deck $2.'

Nearby, a rival steamship company sign invited visitors to take an 'Exciting steamer ride up the Mighty Sacramento River.' Below, a barker dressed in a flashy striped suit waved tickets in the faces of passers-by, urging them not to miss the trip of a lifetime!

As arriving passengers poured from the stationhouse, urchin newspaper boys swarmed around them, shouting the latest headlines. In the street fronting the station horse-drawn streetcars run by the City Railway Company waited to carry arriving passengers into Sacramento. Adding to the traffic jam was a long line of carriages and buckboards filled with impatient passengers, all anxious to board the departing trains and steamers.

Raven couldn't believe her eyes. As Gabriel helped her and her mother off the train, she just stood there on the crowded platform, gaping at the spectacle.

'Mite different than the desert, huh?' Gabriel said to her.

She nodded, speechless. 'Are all cities like this?'

'Some are much bigger,' her mother said. 'As a little girl, when I came over from the old country with my folks, I remember landing in New York and thinking that all the people in the world must live there. Have you ever traveled back east?' she asked Gabriel.

'Nope. Likely never will either. I like my crowds to come one at a time.' Carrying their valises to a bench, he told them to wait for him while he unloaded the Morgan from the boxcar.

'Want me to help?' Raven asked. 'Brandy won't bite me.'

Gabriel ignored her and continued on along the platform to the first of several boxcars that were attached behind the last passenger car. As he approached he saw the conductor standing beside a loading ramp. Two depot workers were on the ramp trying to rope the stallion which was snorting and kicking in the boxcar. A third man stood nearby nursing a bleeding hand.

'Mister,' the conductor said as Gabriel joined him. 'You got just ten seconds to get that muckraker out of there. After that I get someone to shoot him.'

'Do what you gotta do,' Gabriel said. 'I'll do the same.' His hand strayed to his gun. As the conductor jumped back, alarmed, Gabriel signaled to the workmen to get down. They quickly obeyed.

Gabriel walked up the ramp into the car and looked at the Morgan. Eyes blazing red, nostrils flared, it lunged at him.

Gabriel stood his ground. The stallion stopped a few inches from him and bared its teeth. Gabriel felt its hot, rancid breath on his face.

'New territory, new rules,' he told the horse. He dug into his Levi's and pulled out the last of the piñon nuts.

The Morgan eyed the nuts suspiciously then gently ate them out of Gabriel's hand. Gabriel picked up his saddle, threw it over the back of the stallion and cinched it tight. He then grabbed the bridle from a hook, eased the bit into the horse's mouth and fastened the straps.

The conductor and workmen fell back as Gabriel led the Morgan down the ramp toward them. As he passed the man who'd been bitten, Gabriel flipped him a silver dollar.

'Better see the doc 'bout that hand, fella. Hate for you to get infected.'

Stepping into the saddle, Gabriel rode back to Ingrid and Raven. They weren't on the bench and their luggage was gone. He frowned, puzzled, and then heard Raven call out his name.

Turning, he saw her emerge from the stationhouse with her mother. With them was a big, fleshy, handsome man in his early fifties. He wore a black jacket over his gray vest, a white shirt fastened with a string-tie and his black pants were tucked in half boots. Beneath his spotless pearl-gray Stetson his face was square, jut jawed and pugnacious. He had banker's eyes.

Dismounting, Gabriel led his horse up to them.

'Gabe, this is my stepbrother, Reece Blackwood,' Ingrid introduced.

'And you're Mr Moonlight,' Reece said quickly. 'Can't tell you what a pleasure it is to meet you.' He shook Gabriel's hand firmly, chewing as he talked. 'Ingrid's been telling me how kind you've been to her and Raven.'

'More like the other way 'round,' Gabriel said quietly.

'Ingrid said you'd say that.' Reece smiled and Gabriel smelled licorice on his breath. 'But modesty aside, I'm truly grateful to you. And if there's ever anything I can do for you — anything at all — just let me know. They both mean the world to me, as you can imagine.'

Gabriel nodded. He wasn't fully sold on the other's sincerity but decided not to rush to judgment.

'Look what Uncle Reece gave me,' Raven said, holding up a small pale blue package with *Black Jack* printed on it. 'It's called chewing gum. It's the latest fad. Want a piece?'

Gabriel, who'd never seen chewing gum, reluctantly took the stick from Raven, peeled away the tin foil and put the gum in his mouth. His eyebrows arched approvingly. 'Tasty.'

'I chew it all the time,' Reece said. 'Helps keep me relaxed. Trouble is the damn stuff doesn't hold its flavor so I must go through a half-dozen packs a day.'

'Uncle Reece gets boxes of it shipped to him all the way from St. Louis,' Raven told Gabriel.

She went on talking but he'd stopped listening. Behind Reece, Latigo Rawlins had just stepped out of the depot into the sunlight and Gabriel had a hard time hiding his surprise.

Latigo looked equally surprised to see Gabriel and his hands dropped close to his guns as he approached the group.

'Well, well,' he said. 'Small world.'

'You two know each other?' Reece said, surprised.

'We've met,' Gabriel said coldly. He tipped his hat to Ingrid. 'Reckon I'll be ridin' on now.'

'Can't you stay and have lunch with us? Our connection doesn't leave for another two hours.'

'Yes, yes, you must join us,' put in Reece. 'There's a fine restaurant not far from here and — '

'Sorry,' Gabriel said. 'Got a long ride ahead of me.'

'You can't make Carmel by tonight,' Ingrid said, hurt. 'Surely another hour or so won't make a difference.'

'Why don't you take the train?' Reece suggested. 'I'm sure the Southern Pacific or Central Railroad goes to Monterey. From there it's just a short ride.'

'Had my fill of trains,' Gabriel said. He bent down and gave Raven a hug. 'Remember what I told you.'

'Be responsible.'

'That's part of it.'

'An' take care of Momma.'

'Hallelujah.'

She sniffed, fighting tears. 'Will I ever see you again?'

'Count on it, scout.'

He straightened up. Nodded goodbye to Ingrid and Reece. Gave Latigo a curt look. Stepped into the saddle.

'Be nice to Brandy,' Raven called after him.

Gabriel waved to show he'd heard her and rode off.

'Interesting fella,' Reece said.

'If I had a son,' Ingrid said quietly, 'Gabe's how I'd want him to grow up.'

'Nice sentiment. But he belongs in a museum.'

'What do you mean?'

'The world's passed him by.'

'Nonsense. Just because a man wants to ride — '

'I meant he's a gunfighter. Can tell by his eyes. The catlike way he moves. Am I right?' he asked Latigo.

The little gunman shrugged as if he

didn't want to be included.

Reece turned back to Ingrid. 'We'll be in the twentieth century before you know it. His kind will be nothing but a memory, a bad memory, ground under by progress.'

'That include me too, Mr Blackwood?' Latigo said, deadly soft.

'Sure.' Reece popped a fresh stick of gum in his mouth and chewed vigorously. 'You and Moonlight, you're the last of a dying breed.'

20

It took Gabriel three days and three nights to reach the Carmel Valley. He could have reached there sooner but he didn't want to push the Morgan too hard and he also had a lot on his mind.

He kept to the back trails, avoiding towns and people as much as possible and eating off the land. He rode past fragrant peach orchards, vast cattle ranches and farms surrounded by corn fields and acres of vegetables, and, as he got nearer the coast, through forests of oak and pine. Deer and rabbits were everywhere. He shot only what he needed, built a fire where the smoke wouldn't be seen, and ate everything but the bones.

He felt, he thought, as if he'd been reborn.

At night, under an indigo sky bright with stars, he let the Morgan graze at will, spread his bedroll in secluded hollows and lay there smoking and thinking about Ellie and Ingrid and Raven, trying to figure out what place they belonged in his life.

On the afternoon of the third day he reached Monterey Bay. The craggy, dramatic coastline was fogged in. Monterey Pines grew along the clifftops, their twisting gnarly branches poking up through the fog like ghostly skeletons. The weather reminded Gabriel of his childhood when he traveled with his father, a devout circuit preacher, among the gold camps in the Colorado Mountains.

The fog unnerved the Morgan. Gabriel was forced to dismount and lead the skittish stallion until they got farther inland where the sun had burned the fog away. Along the way he stopped and ate wild black berries growing beside the trail.

Ahead, a family of Mexicans was filling baskets with the berries. All the children were girls. The oldest smiled shyly at Gabriel, who politely tipped his hat and asked her for directions to the Mission San Carlos Borromeo de Carmelo. She pointed the way and he nudged the Morgan inland.

He rode over low rolling hills covered with lush grass and scrub bushes and across a valley bright with wild flowers growing among clumps of oak trees. Still within sight of the Pacific Ocean, he finally topped a rise and saw spread out below him a large plain with a river winding through it. A few hovels were scattered along the far bank. Above them on a green hillside was the mission.

Gabriel reined up and looked at it in surprise. It wasn't what he expected; certainly nothing like the well-kept missions in New Mexico and Mexico. There were no other buildings or stables and only the weed-covered ruins of a protective wall remained around the church, which was in sad disrepair. The domed bell tower was cracked and its bell badly rusted by the sea air. The stone walls of the church had crumbled in places and swallows darted in and out of the broken windows. Yet strangely, despite all the deterioration, the slanted shingle roof of the church was relatively new.

A faint sound came from inside the church. At first Gabriel thought it was the wind blowing through the crevices; but as he rode closer he realized it was children singing.

Crossing the river, he dismounted by the arched doorway, tied the Morgan to a stump and entered the church. The interior was equally deteriorated. Wind-blown sand covered the floor along with sprouting grasses and weeds. Rafters and chunks of stone from the old roof blocked his way to the sanctuary and as he picked his way over the debris, squirrels fled underfoot.

The singing, wondrously clear-pitched, was coming from the sacristy. Gabriel peered around a crumbled wall and saw half a dozen shabbily dressed Indian children singing in front of a nun whose face he instantly recognized: it was Ellie!

She saw Gabriel at the same moment. In the midst of conducting the misfit choir she suddenly froze, her expression a mixture of shock and disbelief.

Then she fainted.

The children stopped singing and cowered as they saw Gabriel. Not knowing what tribe they were he spoke to them in Spanish, trying to calm them. But they didn't understand him and fled in all directions.

Picking Ellen up, Gabriel carried her outside. There, he removed her coronet, revealing her close-cropped, pale honey-colored hair, and splashed water on her face from his canteen.

Gradually, she regained consciousness.

'It's OK,' he said as she looked confused. 'Don't be scared, Ellie. It's me — Gabe. Remember?'

''Course I do.' Suddenly she smiled. 'It's just that . . . for a moment, I thought I was seeing a vision.'

'More like a nightmare, you mean.'

She laughed. 'Oh, Gabe, Gabe, I'm so happy to see you.' She threw her arms around his neck and hugged him. 'All this time I thought you were — '

'Dead? Nah. I'm too ornery to die.'

'But when you rode away you looked so weak and pale . . . had lost so much blood . . . I was certain you couldn't last much longer — good gracious!' she said suddenly. 'The children — where are they?'

'They ran off. Reckon they thought I was a vision, too.'

Eager to regain their trust, Ellen led Gabriel to the river and introduced him to the impoverished Indian families living in the hovels. Shy and reclusive, they said little and seemed downtrodden, Gabriel thought. He therefore wasn't surprised when later as he and Ellen returned to the church she explained that these few Indians were all that remained of the once-proud Esselen tribe that in 1771 Father Junipero Serra had recruited to build the hillside mission. Disease and brutality, she said, had all but exterminated them.

Same old story, Gabriel thought

bitterly. Everywhere the padres go they end up killing more Indians than they convert.

Ellen next led Gabriel to the sanctuary garden. 'Father Serra's buried here,' she said, pointing to a tiny weed-strewn grave, 'along with some of his compatriots and all the Indians who died over the centuries.'

'You stay in this pile of ruins, Ellie,' Gabriel said gruffly, 'an' you'll die too.'

'If that's what the Good Lord intended, so be it. I've finally found peace of mind. Can you understand that? All these years I've been trying to find what it is that I was put on earth for and now at last I know.'

'Mean, dyin' for no reason?'

'Oh, but there is a reason — those poor creatures you just met, living in squalor when once they roamed free by the ocean, healthy and happy and in harmony with the earth.'

'An' you, you're supposed to save 'em?'

'It is God's wish,' she said quietly. 'And I'm humbly grateful that He chose someone as lowly as me to do His work.'

Gabriel studied her in the sunlight shining in through a broken window. Her lovely face shone bright with God.

'Please don't be angry with me, Gabe. Just be glad that I'm finally happy.'

He knew then she was out of his reach and stopped trying to make sense of why she was throwing away her life.

'Come,' she took his hand, 'I want to show you where I live. Then no matter where you are, or how far away, you'll be able to close your eyes and see me any time you want.' She led him back into the church and along a corridor to a tiny, bleak cell. 'This was once Father Serra's room and now it's mine.'

Gabriel looked at the barred window with its decrepit wooden shutters, at the bed of boards in the corner and the tarnished silver crucifix hanging on the opposite wall and slowly shook his head.

'I don't expect you to understand,' she said. 'But living here and helping the Esselens has given purpose to my life. I am truly content. And what more can anyone ask for?'

* * *

Early the next morning they walked, hand in hand, along the cliffs and watched the waves breaking on the empty beach below. They did not speak. Cooled by tangy breezes and surrounded by what Ellen called paradise, there seemed to be no need for conversation. Even Gabriel, much as he hated to admit it, felt a sense of serenity he'd never known before.

When it was time for him to leave, Ellen waited until he was in the saddle before asking: 'Where will you go now?'

'Reckon I'll let Brandy, here, decide that.'

'He's certainly changed,' she said, fondling the stallion's nose. 'Not long ago he would've bitten me for touching him.'

'He's gone soft,' Gabriel said. He

reached down and fondly squeezed her shoulder. 'I wish you well, Ellie.'

'Thank you.' She kissed the back of his hand. 'May God be with you wherever you go.'

I'm sure He's got better things to do, Gabriel thought. Tipping his hat, he kicked the Morgan into a canter and rode away without looking back.

* * *

Keeping within sight of the ocean, he headed north trying to convince himself that he didn't know where he was going. But deep down he knew that was a damned lie. He was going where his heart lay: Old Calico.

He'd only ridden a short distance when he realized how boring the Morgan had become. Deciding to fix that, he removed his hat and slapped the stallion over the head with it.

Instantly the startled horse reared up, squealing with rage, and started bucking. Gabriel clung on gamely but was finally thrown to the ground. Dazed, he lay there for a second — only to see the stallion, teeth bared, charging him. He quickly rolled aside and narrowly missed getting stomped.

Jumping up, he stood there laughing. The Morgan circled him, snorting, eyes blazing, and then as if realizing they were back to the old rules, trotted up to him.

'I don't know 'bout you, horse,' Gabriel said, stepping into the saddle, 'but I feel a damn sight better.'

21

Gabriel dismounted beside the creek and let the Morgan slake its thirst. Hunkering down, he filled his canteen, drank his fill, and then splashed water over his sun-and-wind-burned face. Feeling much cooler, he wet his bandanna and knotted it about his throat. He'd been riding since sunup and it was now late afternoon. Most of the trail had been uphill, winding through the rocky hills and canyons, often following the old Southern Pacific branch line that ran from Sacramento to Hangtown, or Placerville as the former gold-rush town was now called.

It had been a hot, tiring ride. But now, according to an old prospector he'd just passed, Old Calico was less than a mile away. Gabriel grasped the reins, avoiding as he did a sly nip by the Morgan, mounted and continued on up the trail. As he rode he wondered what kind of reception awaited him. Would Ingrid and Raven still want him around? Would Reece Blackwood welcome him as readily as he had promised or had his instinct been right when he sensed the banker's friendliness was insincere and he was merely putting on a show for Ingrid?

Shots jolted him back to reality. Gabriel grabbed his Winchester, levered a shell into the chamber and guided the stallion toward some rocks blocking his view of the trail ahead.

Angry shouting reached Gabriel. As he rounded the rocks he saw a young man being dragged behind a galloping rider. Three other riders rode alongside, taunting the victim.

Taking quick aim, Gabriel fired and cut the rope.

Freed of the dragging weight, the horse stumbled and pitched the rider over its head. He landed hard, dazed for a moment, and then jumped up and glared at Gabriel. The other riders, who'd pulled up, angrily turned in their saddles.

'Easy,' Gabriel warned, leveling his rifle at them. 'Caution's the way.'

'Who the hell are you, mister?'

'More to the point,' Gabriel said, 'why're you draggin' that young fella around?'

'That's none of your damn' business,' the oldest of the riders, Gatlin Vogel, said. He had a sheriff's badge pinned to his shirt and Gabriel now noticed the other men wore deputy badges. 'Now, 'fore you dig yourself a grave, ride on an' I'll forget you ever mixed into this.'

Ignoring him, Gabriel rode to the young man. No more than seventeen, he untangled himself from the noose, rose, and slapped the dirt from his ragged, disheveled clothes.

'Anythin' broke?' Gabriel asked him.

'Reckon not.' Under a mop of unkempt red hair there were scratches on his sullen, rebellious face and his dark eyes were full of contempt. 'Don't know why you butted in,' he said grudgingly, 'but I reckon I owe you some thanks.'

'Where's your horse?'

'Harlin, there,' the young man, Mitch Utley, thumbed at one of the deputies, 'shot it out from under me. Else I'd be back in Diablo Canyon by now.'

'Never shoulda left there in the first place,' Sheriff Vogel growled. 'You an' your pa an' the rest of your pig-suckin' brood, you ain't welcome in Old Calico. An' I aim to make all of you remember that.' Turning to Gabriel, he added: 'For the last time, mister — ride on.'

'Be glad to.' Gabriel removed his boot from the stirrup nearest the cowboy and extended his hand. 'Jump up, boy.'

Mitch swung up behind Gabriel. Keeping his eye on the sheriff and his deputies, Gabriel backed up the Morgan until they reached the trail and then rode off.

Ahead, the trail snaked down into a deep, broad canyon. Snuggled between the steep rocky slopes, most of which were scarred with abandoned mines, was Old Calico. It looked no different than most small towns that had been founded during the gold rush — except for one difference: when the mines finally played out and gold became scarcer than an honest man, thanks to the railroad Old Calico had managed to survive.

And now, thirty years later, it was thriving and prosperous.

Gabriel slowed the Morgan to a walk and rode between two rows of neatly painted false-front stores facing each other across a paved street. Both sidewalks were also paved and hanging on poles were electric arc lamps powered by dynamos. Side streets led back to well-kept two-story, wood-frame houses and as Gabriel reined up in front of the bank, the people on the sidewalk looked at Mitch as if he were a leper.

'Don't look like you're too popular,' Gabriel said dryly as he and Mitch dismounted.

'That's 'cause I ain't one of 'em. An' if you're goin' in there,' Mitch said, meaning the bank, 'I ain't one of you neither.'

'One of who?'

'Miner trash!' a woman yelled at Mitch as she and her husband rode past in a wagon. 'Get back where you belong!'

'Reckon that answers my question,' Gabriel said.

'Mine, too,' Mitch said. 'Only thing I can't figure out is if you're one of Blackwood's new guns, why'd you help me back there?'

Gabriel gave a wolfish smile. ''Fore you hang a sign on someone, boy, might be wise to know who he is.' Slinging his saddle-bags over his shoulder, he entered the bank.

Inside, everything was clean, well-appointed and orderly. Gabriel looked at the well-dressed customers doing business at the teller windows and wished he'd shaved and bathed before looking up Ingrid's stepbrother. But it was too late. Coming out of his office toward him was Reece Blackwood and the handsome little gunfighter from Texas, Latigo Rawlins.

'What'd I tell you,' Gabriel heard Latigo mutter. 'He's harder to lose than a plugged nickel.'

Reece ignored him. Smiling, he stuck out his hand to Gabriel and said: 'Glad you took me up on my offer, Mr Moonlight. Can always use a good man.'

Gabriel didn't remember any offer but said anyway: 'Thanks, but I'm not lookin' for work.'

'Then you must be looking for my stepsister.' Reece put a fresh stick of Black Jack gum in his mouth. 'Your timing's perfect. I'm just heading home so I'll let her know you're here. I can't wait to see the look on her face when she sees you. You'll stay for dinner of course? Seven o'clock suit you?' He turned to Latigo. 'Tell Mr Moonlight how to get to my house.' He was gone, the door swinging shut behind him before either Gabriel or Latigo could say anything.

'He ever wait for an answer?' Gabriel said wryly.

'Not unless it comes out of his mouth,' Latigo said.

22

The Blackwood Mansion, as it was known, sat on a low grassy rise at the end of the canyon. Three stories of wood and stone with a slate roof, a wedding cake façade and a large front porch overlooking the valley beyond, it was the envy of everyone in Old Calico. The furniture was handmade in San Francisco, the paintings by famous American and European artists and each room was lit by dynamo-charged electricity. That wasn't all. The china, crystal and silverware came from Europe; and the snowy tablecloth was made of the finest Irish linen.

Gabriel, now bathed and shaved, was extra careful during dinner so that he didn't spill anything on it.

Ingrid, sensing his unease, kept the conversation light and breezy; and to make sure he wasn't embarrassed by using the incorrect silverware, she made sure before each course was served by the icy-polite British butler that Gabriel saw which knife, fork or spoon she was using.

As the five-course meal ended and cigars were brought out, Raven entered to say goodnight. Resentful of Reece's strict rules — one of which was that 'children' did not dine with 'grown-ups' when guests were invited — she kissed her mother fondly, grudgingly muttered goodnight to 'Uncle Reece,' and made a big fuss about fawning over Gabriel and telling him how much she'd missed him.

'I'm envious,' Reece half-joked to Gabriel after Raven had left. 'She seems to really like you.'

'No more than she does you,' Ingrid said quickly.

'I'd like to think that,' he said. 'But there are times, many times, when I get the feeling she's avoiding me.'

'Nonsense. Raven's not like that. She's entirely honest about her feelings.

If she didn't like you, she'd tell you. Isn't that right, Gabe?'

'She's not shy 'bout speakin' her piece,' Gabriel agreed. Inwardly, though, he knew something was wrong. From the moment he'd arrived he could tell Raven wasn't happy. The way she hugged him and remained at his side, ignoring Reece, made it obvious that she disliked him.

'She doesn't even ask me for chewing gum anymore,' Reece said, hurt. 'And when I offered to buy her a new dress the other day, she pretended not to hear me. Do you think it's something I've done, or said to her?' he asked Ingrid. Before she could answer, the butler entered. He spoke quietly to Reece, who immediately frowned and gave Gabriel a hard look.

'Excuse me,' he said, rising. 'I'll only be a minute.'

When he'd left Ingrid quickly turned to Gabriel. 'I'm worried, Gabe. Reece is right. Raven does seem to have turned against him.'

'Maybe she resents bein' bossed around by a stranger.'

'But he's not a stranger; he's her uncle. And after all, this is his home so it's only proper that she do as he asks.'

''Cause it's proper doesn't make it easier to swallow.'

Ingrid didn't answer for a moment. 'I've tried to discuss it with her,' she said finally. 'But it was like talking to a stone wall. You like him, don't you?' she said when Gabriel didn't respond.

'Don't dislike him.'

'That's not what I asked you.'

'It's my answer.'

'In other words, you won't discuss it? My God, you are so exasperating,' she said when again he didn't respond. 'It's no wonder Raven adores you. You're two of a kind — '

She broke off as her brother returned. Apologizing for his absence, he put fresh gum in his mouth and asked Ingrid if he could have a moment alone with Gabriel.

'Of course.' Rising, she gathered up

her cream satin gown so she wouldn't trip on the flowing skirt and withdrew.

Reece poured Gabriel a brandy and came right to the point: 'That was Sheriff Vogel. Seems you and he had a little misunderstanding earlier.'

'That what he called it?'

Reece Blackwood sighed, spat his licorice gum into a brass spittoon and reached for a cigar. 'I'm not going to lie to you, Gabe. What you saw wasn't pleasant but it was necessary. It's the only kind of treatment the Utleys understand.' He paused, expecting Gabriel to say something. When he didn't, Reece said: 'I don't condone Vogel's barbaric actions but nor do I intend to reprimand him for them either. They get results. And right now, I need results.'

'Must be a better way than draggin' a boy in the dirt.'

'That boy,' Reece said angrily, 'is part of a clan of human filth that lives — no, make that infests — Diablo Canyon. They're like a plague. They live like animals and multiply like vermin, fouling everything they touch. Their leader's a violent, bullying patriarch who goes by the name of Remus Utley.'

'The boy's kin?'

'His father.' Reece clipped the end off his cigar and lit it with a gold lighter. 'He's an illiterate drunk who beats his wife and sires children like they were rats. Remus's grandfather, Eli, spent what little gold he found in whore houses and died of syphilis and the father was killed in a mine cave-in. Everyone expected Remus to move the clan out of the canyon after that, but he didn't. Instead he spread out into Rockfall Pass. I offered him a more than fair price for the land but he laughed in my face. Said he intended to stay there till he rotted to death.'

'Why? Is there gold or silver to be dug out?'

'Not a dime's worth. Even in the gold rush days it was known as Dry Diggin's. That's what's so crazy about this whole thing. To spite me — well, the townspeople,' Reece corrected, 'he's brought pain and misery to not only his own family but the half-dozen other families who live there with him. God knows, I've done everything a civilized man could possibly do to make him change his mind. But it's useless. He'd rather see everyone starve to death than give up his land.'

Gabriel eyed Reece shrewdly and spit out a stream of smoke. 'If the land ain't worth anythin', why do you want it?'

'I don't. I just want them out of there. Filth like that spreads like a disease. Gives Old Calico a bad name and stops outsiders from coming here. And without outsiders, no town can exist for long. And I don't intend for scum like the Utleys to destroy something I've nurtured into prosperity, something good, a town where decent folks can live and work and raise their families in safety — '

'So you resorted to force?'

'I had no other choice. As I said, I've offered Remus money, land — fertile

204

land where he and his clan could relocate — all to no avail. So now I intend to drive him out, by any means available to me — '

'Includin' Latigo Rawlins?'

'Including Latigo Rawlins. I don't know why that should disgust you,' Reece said, seeing Gabriel's expression. 'Latigo isn't doing anything you didn't do back when you were on the prod for Stillman Stadtlander.'

Gabriel smiled unpleasantly and studied the smoke curling up from his cigar. 'Was wonderin' when you'd get around to that.'

'Don't worry. I don't intend to tell Ingrid.'

'No need. She an' Raven already know what I was — still am when it comes right down to it.'

Reece looked surprised but didn't say anything. The two men smoked in silence for a few moments.

'So what can I expect?' Reece said finally. 'More of the same or are you going to back my play?'

'Anyone who isn't with you is against you, that it?'

'Isn't that how you'd look at it?'

Gabriel slowly got to his feet. 'Blackwood, let's get somethin' straight. My gun's not for sale.'

Reece watched Gabriel walk to the door. There was something lethal about the man and it scared him.

'You don't like me much, do you, Moonlight?'

'I don't like you at all,' Gabriel said. He walked out.

Ingrid was coming down the stairs as he collected his hat from the blank-faced butler.

'You're leaving?'

He nodded. She saw a glint in his eyes that troubled her.

'You and my brother, you had words?'

Again, he nodded.

'About me?'

'Ask him. G'night.'

'Wait. Will I see you again?'

'I'll be around.' He left. The butler

closed the door and returned to the kitchen.

Ingrid felt someone watching. Turning, she saw Reece standing in the dining room door.

'What did you two argue about?'

'He didn't tell you?'

'Said to ask you.'

'I wanted him to side with me against the Utleys. There's big trouble looming, sis, and I could use his gun.'

'Good God,' Ingrid said. 'You invite him to dinner and then ask him to kill for you?'

'It's what gunfighters do, in case you've forgotten.'

'But not bankers,' she said scathingly, 'in case *you've* forgotten!' She stormed upstairs.

'Ingrid!' Reece went to the foot of the stairs and called after his stepsister. 'Ingrid, wait — I want to talk to you.'

She ignored him and he heard her bedroom door slam.

'Well, well,' a low voice said mockingly. 'Trouble in paradise?'

Reece whirled and saw Latigo standing in the kitchen doorway, munching on a chicken leg.

'Get out of my house!' Reece shouted at him.

The small, slim gunfighter grinned impudently, tossed the chicken leg over his shoulder into the kitchen, licked his fingers clean and strolled past Reece to the front door.

There he turned and said softly: 'Don't ever raise your voice to me again, Mr Blackwood. Or I might forget I work for you.' He walked out and down the steps to his horse.

Enraged, Reece grabbed an ancient Grecian urn sitting atop a small antique table, and hurled it against the wall.

It shattered into a thousand pieces.

23

Gabriel awoke with a start. It wasn't yet dawn and someone was pounding on his hotel door.

'Moonlight — Moonlight, you in there?'

Recognizing Reece Blackwood's voice, Gabriel thumbed the hammer back on his Colt and went to the door. 'What do you want?'

'Open up!'

'I can hear you through the door.'

'Damn you, it's important! Remus Utley's kidnapped Ingrid and Raven — '

Gabriel yanked open the door and saw Reece, armed with a shotgun, and behind him Latigo Rawlins.

'When?'

'Some time earlier tonight.'

'Know where he's taken them?'

'Diablo Canyon, most likely.'

'It's payback,' Latigo added. 'For

what Sheriff Vogel an' his deputies did to his boy, Mitch.'

'Will you throw in with us now?' Reece said.

Nodding, Gabriel sat on the bed, quickly pulled on his boots and shirt and buckled on his gun-belt. 'How'd this Utley fella get hold of 'em?'

'Some of his men broke into my home, pistol-whipped the butler and snatched them right out of their bedrooms.'

'You must sleep heavy.'

'Normally I would've heard them,' Reece said, ashamed. 'But after you left I drank more than I should've, and — ' He left the rest unsaid.

'Any idea what Utley intends on doin' with them?'

'No. I doubt if he'll harm them — even Remus can't be that crazy. He knows he'd have everyone in the territory down on him. But other than that, I've no idea. I do know this, though,' Reece said grimly. 'This is the last time that bastard's ever going to make me sweat. Once Ingrid and Raven are safe, I'm going to wipe him and his ugly brood out, once and for all!'

Finished dressing, Gabriel grabbed his hat and followed Reece and Latigo down the stairs. Outside the hotel Sheriff Vogel, his deputies and some thirty armed riders waited.

One of them held the reins belonging to a big rangy buckskin. 'The hostler couldn't get your horse out of the stall,' he explained to Gabriel. 'Says the ornery devil tried to bite him every time he got close.'

'Sounds 'bout right,' said Gabriel. 'Got a mean streak in him wider'n the Red River.' Climbing into the saddle, he spurred the buckskin into a gallop and rode after Reece, Latigo and the others.

★　★　★

Ten minutes of hard riding brought the posse to the mouth of Rockfall Pass — a narrow, steep-walled gap in the hills that had earned its name twenty years earlier when an earthquake caused a rock slide that buried a group of miners on their way to Placerville.

Reece gathered everyone around him and spoke to the sheriff. 'I want this done legally. Swear everyone in. That way, no one can ever accuse us of vigilantism.'

'You heard Mr Blackwood, boys. Now raise your right hand an' swear to uphold the law, so help you God.'

Everyone but Gabriel and Latigo obeyed. Sheriff Vogel knew better than to press them. 'It's done, Mr Blackwood.'

Satisfied, Reece faced the men. 'Okay, now listen up. There're lots of women and children in there. I don't want any of them harmed. That clear?'

'Them's Utley women, boss,' a rider grumbled. 'They ain't gonna just stand there while we gun down their men.'

'That's different. If any of them shoot at you, shoot back. You two,' Reece added to Gabriel and Latigo, 'stick with me. Remus is most likely holding Ingrid and Raven hostage in his cabin. While the men keep Utley's boys pinned down, it's up to us to get them out of there.'

'This Utley,' Gabriel said, 'he some kinda fool?'

'Far from it. He's cunning as a snake.'

'Then he'll be expectin' us. We go bustin' in there an' he'll cut us down long before we can get to the women.'

'Not if we strike now. If he's expecting us at all, it won't be till daylight. There're hundreds of places to hide in the pass and the canyon and the Utleys know every one of them. Remus won't think anyone would dare attack him in the dark.'

'An' if you're wrong?'

'Then we'll force his hand and shoot it out. I'd take these men against a bunch of Utley trash any day.'

'Not arguin' that.'

'Then what's eating you?'

'I'm worried about Ingrid an' Raven. You willin' to risk their lives on a hunch? If Utley's the kind of filth you been paintin' him, an' he knows a rope's waitin' for him, what's to stop him from shootin' both of them just out of spite?'

Reece realized Gabriel was right. 'You have a better idea?'

'I ride in alone. Utley doesn't know me, but his boy, Mitch, does. Maybe he'll remember I cut him loose an' saved him some roughing up by the sheriff. If he does, could be I can persuade him to make his old man listen to reason.'

'And if you can't?'

'You'll have a gun on the inside and I'll be usin' it to protect Ingrid and Raven when you come bustin' in.'

Reece Blackwood mulled over Gabriel's offer then took out his fob watch and checked the time. 'Sunup's in two hours. Another fifteen minutes for the sun to climb high enough to clear the ridgeline and bring daylight to the canyon. That's how long you've got to talk Remus into letting the women go.'

'Hold it,' Sheriff Vogel said. 'Puttin' a lotta trust in this stranger, aren't you, Mr Blackwood?'

'Meaning?'

'What if Utley hired him to come here? The ol' man's been threatenin' to bring in outside guns for weeks now. Mebbe he's one of 'em.'

'That's nonsense. He came to see my stepsister.'

'Mebbe. An' mebbe that was just his cover.'

Silence.

The men looked suspiciously at Gabriel, who made no attempt to deny the accusation.

'It would explain why he cut Mitch loose an' why he's so all-fired on goin' in there alone. Hell, he's probably just itchin' to warn Remus we're comin' in.'

Angry, the men started muttering in agreement.

And still Gabriel said nothing.

'At least deny it,' Reece said to him.

'Why should he?' Latigo put in. 'He knows it ain't true.' He turned to the sheriff beside him. 'An' he knows you got pig slop for brains.'

Sheriff Vogel reddened angrily. 'An' you got a big mouth, Shorty — ' He broke off, alarmed, as he felt something pressing against his chin — and realized it was one of Latigo's ivory-handled, nickel-plated guns.

Gabriel, accustomed as he was to gunmen with quick reflexes, had never seen anyone draw so fast.

'Easy,' he said softly. 'Caution's the way.'

Latigo showed no sign of hearing him. Rage narrowed his eyes into twin yellow slits.

'Let it go, Rawlins,' Reece pleaded. 'One shot could mean the end for my stepsister and niece.'

For another second Latigo seemed on the verge of shooting the sheriff. Then he smiled, boyishly, and returned the gun to its holster — only slightly slower than he'd drawn it.

'You're a lucky fella, Sheriff. But if you wanna enjoy your rockin'-chair days, don't ever call me that again.' He turned his horse away and Sheriff Vogel sagged with relief.

'Go ahead,' Reece told Gabriel. 'But remember: in two hours we're coming in.'

24

As Gabriel rode into the eerie shadows of Rockfall Pass he kept his hands away from his guns. Nor did he attempt to watch for lookouts hiding in the steep, rocky slopes on both sides of him. There was no point. The trail was hard and stony and he knew if anyone was there they could hear the stallion coming.

Now and then he heard loose stones falling as someone moved above him; and once, when the moon poked through the clouds, he glimpsed the silhouette of a man with a rifle leaping from rock to rock as he descended the slope.

So, Gabriel thought, they don't plan on shooting me yet.

After a mile or so the pass widened and became a bowl-shaped canyon sheltered by towering red cliffs. In the moonlight the cliffs looked silver; but in sunlight they glowed like the fires of hell prompting the Mexicans who originally discovered the area to call it: *El Cañon del Diablo*.

Gabriel slowed the buckskin to a walk and entered the canyon. To his right a creek snaked out of the rocks in front of a collection of rundown shacks, barns and corrals. On the slopes above the shacks were the entrances to numerous abandoned mines — and out of every mine poked at least one rifle, sometimes three or four.

Gabriel kept both hands on the reins so no one could misinterpret his intentions and guided his horse toward the largest of the shacks.

As he drew near two men emerged. Gabriel recognized one as Mitch, the young man he'd rescued from the sheriff. The other he hadn't seen before — but he knew from now on he'd never forget him.

Bald, red-bearded and ferocious-looking in an undershirt and pants he was easily the largest man Gabriel had ever seen. He towered over his son, who Gabriel remembered was about six feet, and his girth was larger around than a whiskey barrel. He was so large in fact that as Gabriel reined up in front of the shack he saw that the door had been specially widened in order for the man to squeeze through.

'Is it him?' the huge man asked Mitch.

'Yep.'

'Sure now?'

'Yeah, Pa. He's ridin' a different horse but it's him all right.' Mitch looked up at Gabriel. 'You got sand comin' in here alone, mister. If I hadn'ta recognized you in the pass you'd be crow meat by now.'

'So that was you with the rifle.'

'You seen me?' Mitch said, surprised.

'Judas,' the huge man said, cuffing him. 'I taught you better'n that.'

'He's lyin', Pa,' Mitch said, sulking.

'No, son. I saw you all right,' Gabriel said. 'Once. When the moon was right.' He turned to the huge man. 'You must

220

be Remus Utley?'

'What of it, mister?'

'Expected you to have horns.'

Remus cocked his massive head and squinted at Gabriel as if sizing him up.

'You just jawin' or you got somethin' worthwhile to spit out?'

'I talk better when I'm afoot.'

Remus groped under his enormous belly and brought out a pistol that looked tiny in his meaty fist. Gabriel guessed it must have been stuck in the man's shabby brown pants and wondered if he should risk going for his gun.

'Slide down,' Remus said, his voice a low rumble. Then as Gabriel slowly dismounted: 'Give me your word you ain't here to shoot us an' you can keep your iron.'

'You got it.'

'Pa,' Mitch exclaimed as his father tucked his pistol away, 'how you know you can trust him?'

Remus Utley grinned at Gabriel, showing rotted teeth. 'Make your play.'

Gabriel's right hand moved with blurring speed. One instant it was empty, the next it was aiming his Colt at Remus. Then, even as Mitch gaped, the gun was back in its holster.

Remus cuffed his son on the head. 'Now do you get it?'

Mitch backed away, grumbling: 'Pa, I told you not to keep on hittin' me like that.'

'Look into a man's eyes,' Remus said. 'If you don't see fear where there should be fear, it's 'cause he's holdin' all the aces. Now, speak your piece,' he told Gabriel.

'The woman an' girl . . . I've come for them.'

'Then you've come for nothin'.'

'This ain't their fight.'

'They're Reece Blackwood's kin, ain't they?'

'So it is payback?'

'Do unto others . . . '

'Now who's doin' the jawin'?'

'You're wastin' your breath,' began Mitch.

'Shut up, boy.' Remus wiped his nose on his sweat-stained undershirt and glared at Gabriel. 'You're right. Using a woman and a girl as payback is a foul thing to do. Makes me sick to think I stooped that low. But I got no choice. Mr High an' Mighty Blackwood made sure of that . . . him an' his dirty lies. Made me out to be the devil incarnate. Got folks hatin' us so bad we daren't go to town for supplies or to even take our young'uns in to get proper schoolin'. An' when we tried to board a train for Placerville, to buy food there, the sheriff and his gunmen threatened to rape our women if they ever saw 'em again. Lord knows, I tried to reason with Blackwood but all he can see is railroad money — '

'Railroad money?'

'Southern Pacific wants to build a spur that'd link up to Carson City. Said layin' track through the pass and Diablo Canyon 'stead of blasting through the mountains would save millions. Offered Blackwood a fortune if he'd make us leave.'

Suddenly it all made sense to Gabriel. Reece was motivated by greed; he was looking to line his pockets, not help the citizens of Old Calico.

Gabriel thought a moment and then had an idea. 'What if the SP agreed to pay you instead of Blackwood — would you'n your people move out then?'

'Why would they wanna do a fool thing like that?'

''Cause you threaten to dynamite the pass if they don't. Wouldn't take much — few sticks planted in the right places an' there'd be a landslide that'd take 'em months to blast through. Once you tell 'em that, they'll beg you to take their money.'

He expected Remus to jump at the offer. Instead, the huge man laughed in his face. 'You must think I'm a damn' fool, mister.'

'Pa's right,' Mitch said. 'Railroads don't pay folks like us to do anythin'. They don't have to. They know they can run roughshod over us an' we can't do nothin' about it.'

Gabriel ignored him. 'You didn't answer my question,' he said to Remus.

'It ain't worth answerin'. Now, hit that saddle an' ride outta here.

'Not till I see the woman and girl,' Gabriel said.

Remus hesitated, saw something in the gunfighter's ice-blue eyes that changed his mind, and turned to his son.

'Bring 'em out, boy.'

Gabriel waited until Mitch hurried into the shack then said quietly: 'For a while there, Utley, you had me fooled.'

'Keep talkin'.'

'You're no better'n Blackwood.'

'Watch your mouth, mister.'

'This hate you got for him — it's not about bein' forced off your land or protectin' your people or gettin' proper schoolin' for your young'uns — '

'No? Then what is it about?'

'Windmills,' said Gabriel.

Remus scowled, confused. 'Windmills?'

'Pride. Provin' a point. Slayin' dragons — ' Gabriel broke off as Mitch reappeared with Ingrid and Raven.

Both looked happily astonished to see him. Raven gave a little gasp of joy and ran and hugged him.

'I knew you'd come for us,' she said. 'I just knew it!'

Gabriel fondly tousled her hair and smiled at Ingrid.

'You all right?'

'Fine,' she said. She stepped into his extended arm and let him hold her.

'Time's up,' Remus told Gabriel. 'You've seen 'em. Now get on your horse an' go tell Blackwood to ride on in. I'm waitin' for him.' He turned to Mitch. 'Take 'em inside, boy.'

Gabriel's gun leaped into his hand and pointed at Remus.

The huge man didn't flinch. Instead he whistled and instantly a dozen men with rifles jumped up from behind the rocks around them.

'Your call,' he told Gabriel.

'You'n your boy'll die before I do.'

'So will they,' Remus said, meaning Ingrid and Raven.

Gabriel played his last ace. 'I'm stayin' here with 'em.'

'Not till you hand over your iron.'

Gabriel spun the Colt on his trigger finger and handed it, butt first, to Utley.

Remus tossed the gun to Mitch. 'Take 'em inside an' make sure they don't go nowhere.'

'But Pa, I wanna fight with you.'

Remus cuffed him. 'Do as I say, boy.'

Mitch glared sullenly at him. 'What if you don't win, Pa? What if Blackwood kills you 'stead of the other way 'round?'

'Day that happens,' Remus said, 'you're gonna have to learn to make decisions on your own. Now get inside!'

He waited until Mitch led Gabriel and the women into the shack; then he told his men to mount up. As they ran to the corral, he signaled to the others hiding in the mine entrances and yelled for them to come on down!

The hate that had been burning in his belly for years was finally about to be satisfied.

25

Dawn was slowly yellowing the gray, overcast sky.

Sheriff Vogel ground out his smoke, got to his feet, stretched the stiffness from his muscles and told the men resting around him to saddle up.

He then joined Reece Blackwood, who stood by himself, staring at the narrow entrance to Rockfall Pass.

'Sun's clear of the hills.'

Reece nodded and wadded fresh gum into his mouth.

'You still of a mind to ride in?'

'I say anything to make you think differently?'

'Just wanted to make sure,' Sheriff Vogel said. 'This ain't gonna be no picnic, you know.'

'Nothing I've ever wanted was,' Reece replied. The two men walked to their horses. 'Folks say I'm lucky; that I only trip over four-leaf clovers and prosperity lands in my lap. They couldn't be farther from the truth. I've had to sell my soul to the devil many times.'

'I don't doubt that,' Sheriff Vogel said. There was a sting to his voice that made Reece look sharply at him.

'You don't think much of me, do you, Sheriff?'

The big lawman spat tobacco juice between his horse's hoofs. 'Life ain't a popularity contest, Mr Blackwood. But so long as you keep on payin' me, I reckon you're the nicest fella I know.'

Reece chuckled despite himself. 'Well, at least you're honest, Sheriff. I'll give you that.' He looked about him. 'Where's Latigo?'

The sheriff searched the faces of the riders gathered before him. 'Any of you seen Rawlins?'

The men stood up in their stirrups and looked around.

'Ain't here,' one rider said.

'What do you mean, he's not here?' Reece rode into the pack of riders, his horse shouldering their mounts aside. 'Where the hell is he then?'

The riders looked at each other and shrugged.

'Must've ridden off while we were restin',' Sheriff Vogel said. He shook his head in disgust. 'Never did trust that little sawed-off runt.'

Reece saw a growing uneasiness in the eyes of several of the riders and knew he had to rally them or call off the fight.

'Good riddance to him,' he said. 'Means the rest of you get to divvy up the thousand dollars I promised him. C'mon, Sheriff,' he added, before the men could get over their surprise, 'let's ride.' He spurred his horse forward, the sheriff and his deputies following.

* * *

Gabriel sat smoking in an old rocker. Through half-shut eyes he studied Ingrid and Raven, who lay on the bed opposite him.

230

'She asleep?' he whispered to Ingrid.

She nodded and gently kissed her daughter on the top of her raven-black head.

'Just like she hasn't a care in the world.'

'That's 'cause she trusts you.'

'Trusts *you*, you mean.' When he didn't say anything, she added: 'What's going to happen to us, Gabe?'

'We're gonna be fine.'

'Don't patronize me. Tell me what you really think.'

Before he could answer gunfire broke out.

'There's your answer,' he told her.

'Oh-dear-God,' she said softly.

'Sounds like it's comin' from the pass,' Gabriel said as the shooting increased. 'From what I saw ridin' in, the Utleys most likely got your stepbrother an' his men pinned down.' He saw her wince and wished he'd kept his mouth shut.

Raven now waked with a start. Hearing the steady crackle of rifle fire, she sat up and looked about her as if not sure where she was. 'Momma — who's shooting?'

'It's your Uncle Reece. He and the sheriff and some men are trying to get us out of here.'

'Shouldn't take 'em long,' Gabriel lied.

The door swung open and Mitch stood looking at them, rifle in one hand, Gabriel's Colt in the other.

'I'm goin' to help Pa,' he told Gabriel.

'He said for you to stay here.'

'Don't care what he said. I ain't waitin' no longer. Pa needs me even if he won't admit it. Here,' he tossed the Peacemaker to Gabriel. 'Fend for yourself. I owe you that much.' Turning, he ran out of the shack.

'Too bad,' Gabriel said as they heard Mitch ride off. 'Boy had potential.'

'Now what?' Ingrid asked.

'Got two options,' Gabriel said. 'Wait here till the fightin' stops, which could be a spell, or try to make it over one of the cliffs behind us an' — '

Suddenly, the earth shook.

The ground under the shack heaved so violently, Gabriel, Ingrid and Raven were thrown to the floor.

Furniture overturned. Windows shattered. Pots and pans and dishes fell off hooks and shelves in the kitchen and rolled, clattering, everywhere.

Outside, there was a loud, wrenching, screeching sound as wood and nails were ripped apart. Moments later the porch collapsed.

The shaking seemed to last forever.

Still on the bedroom floor, Gabriel dragged Ingrid and Raven to the overturned bed, grabbed the mattress and pulled it over them. He felt them trembling and gently tried to calm their fears, assuring them that they were safe and that the quake wouldn't last long.

And still the earth shook.

The three of them waited, eyes closed, teeth clinched, bodies tensed, jolted around like corks at sea.

Then, as suddenly as it started, the

shaking stopped.

Everything was still. Silent.

It was, Gabriel thought, as if the earth was holding its breath.

'Thank God,' whispered Ingrid. 'It's over.'

Then the after-shock struck.

It lasted only a few seconds. But in that time the shack was torn loose from the ground. The walls split apart. The roof caved in. The shack collapsed like a house of cards.

26

In Rockfall Pass things were much worse. The earthquake and after-shock had undermined the cliffs on both sides of the trail, splitting them apart. They collapsed, causing twin landslides that buried Reece, Sheriff Vogel and most of the deputies under thousands of tons of rock and dirt.

The Utley forces, hidden among the rocks on the cliffs, fared no better. Unable to save themselves, they were trapped in the landslide and soon buried alongside their enemies in one colossal, enigmatic grave.

The screams of the dying and injured gradually lessened. So did the clouds of falling dust. Finally, only a few painful groans could be heard. And eventually, they too ceased.

There were few survivors.

Buried under the collapsed cabin, Gabriel, Ingrid and Raven heard the thunderous roar of the two landslides.

The silence that followed was almost as deafening.

'Dear mother of God,' Ingrid breathed. 'What was that?'

'Nature,' Gabriel said grimly. 'Reckon she's decided to put an end to this feud herself.' Crawling out from under the mattress, he cleared a hole in the mass of debris overhead and pulled Ingrid and Raven to safety. Other than a few scratches, none of them was hurt. They looked toward the pass but could see nothing but a cloud of swirling dust.

Anxious to get out of the canyon in case another quake hit, Gabriel hurried to the corral. Two unsaddled horses stood huddled together against the fence. Frightened by the quake, they shied away from him. Grabbing a lariat from a post, he entered the corral and spoke gently to them. It took a while but gradually they calmed down. He then roped one for himself and let Ingrid and Raven ride double on his saddled buckskin.

As they approached the blocked pass the still-settling dust hid the few remaining survivors who were frantically digging among the rocks. But it didn't hide the wailing coming from the widows looking for their husbands, or the sobbing of their children.

'You'n Raven stay here,' Gabriel told Ingrid, 'while I look around for — '

She cut him off. 'No, no, I'm going with you!'

'Wouldn't advise that.'

'I'm still going,' she said, fighting not to panic. 'I have to find out if Reece is all right!'

'An' you can forget about leaving me behind,' Raven chimed in. ''Cause nothing you say is gonna make me stay here by myself.'

Gabriel shrugged, 'Suit yourselves,' nudged his horse onward and led them to the pass.

When they were almost to the narrow, rock-strewn entrance, the massive figure of Remus Utley appeared out of the dust. Bruised and bleeding, he staggered toward them carrying a corpse in his arms.

It was Mitch, Gabriel realized, crushed almost beyond recognition. Feeling a tug of regret, he started to offer his condolences. But the huge man lumbered past him without speaking or looking up. Swallowing his remorse, Gabriel dismounted alongside Ingrid and Raven.

'That poor man,' Ingrid whispered sadly. 'How's he ever going to live with himself?'

'He'll survive,' Gabriel said bluntly. 'His kind always does.'

For the next two hours the three of them clambered over the mountain of rocks and dirt looking for Reece. Soon their nails were broken and their hands cut and bleeding. But there was no trace of Ingrid's brother. Still they searched. The sun blazed down remorselessly. Gabriel knew they were wasting their time, but he kept his thoughts to himself and continued looking.

'Momma, we're never going to find him,' Raven said finally. 'Uncle Reece is dead and — '

'We don't know that for certain,' Ingrid snapped. 'And until we do, I'm going to keep looking for him. He's my stepbrother,' she added defensively to Gabriel. 'I must know if he's alive or dead. Surely you can understand that.' Desperate, she continued searching.

Gabriel gently squeezed Raven's shoulder and smiled encouragingly at her. She sensed he was trying to make her understand what her mother was going through, and reluctantly went on looking among the rocks.

★ ★ ★

The sun was directly overhead when Gabriel found Reece Blackwood. His body lay mangled between two boulders, about halfway into the pass, and by his agonized expression Gabriel

239

knew he had not died quickly or without pain.

He looked behind him and saw Ingrid tending to an injured, raggedly dressed Utley woman. Covered in cuts and bruises, she looked dazed and was still clutching her pistol. Nearby, Raven was giving one of the deputies a drink from a canteen she'd found among the rocks. His chest was crushed and he wheezed with pain.

Struggling with his conscience, Gabriel finally decided Ingrid had a right to know her brother was dead and brought her over to the corpse.

She tried to control her emotions but it was too much for her and she broke into tears. Kneeling beside Reece, she gently brushed the dirt from his face, wiped the dribble of licorice chewing gum from his lips and tearfully kissed his cheek. As she did a second, smaller after-shock brought another section of the cliff crashing down around them.

Gabriel grabbed Ingrid's hand and they scrambled over the rocks to Raven.

She was staring at the deputy's corpse, seemingly unaware of the impending danger.

'He's dead,' she said in a tiny, lost voice. 'I was giving him a drink and he . . . he just died.'

'C'mon,' Gabriel grasped their hands and pulled them away. 'Hurry or we'll be buried ourselves.'

Ingrid balked, reluctant to leave her brother's corpse. 'I c-can't just leave him here,' she sobbed. 'He deserves a proper b-burial and — '

More rocks and dirt showered down behind them. They were followed almost immediately by a larger landslide, this one burying Reece's body beneath it.

Gabriel draped his arms around Ingrid and Raven, trying to protect them from flying debris, at the same time shouting that they had to get out of there! 'Dammit, woman, I mean it,' he yelled when Ingrid didn't move. 'We have to go — now!'

As if to remind them of the imminent

danger, the earth again shuddered, bringing down another rockfall.

Still Ingrid refused to leave.

'Please, Momma,' Raven begged. 'I already lost Daddy. I don't want to lose anyone else I love.'

Ingrid heard the fear in her voice and finally relenting, hugged Raven to her. 'All right, lamb. We'll go.'

27

It took them all afternoon to reach the other end of the pass. By then they were exhausted. But Gabriel wouldn't let the women rest. It was still several miles to town, he reminded them, and walking in the dark could be dangerous.

'I'm not walking anywhere,' Raven said. 'Not when there're horses around.' She pointed to a nearby hillside where three of the horses belonging to Sheriff Vogel's deputies — horses that had escaped the landslide — were grazing. 'Want to help me catch 'em?' she said to Gabriel.

Tired as he was, her impudence made him smile. 'You got gall,' he said. 'I'll give you that.' But he went with her anyway.

The earthquake had scared the horses, making them wary, but between them Gabriel and Raven managed to coax two of them close enough to grab their reins. Giving Ingrid and Raven the placid-looking bay, Gabriel took the skittish roan and they wearily headed toward town.

Ingrid rode in silence. All cried out, she stared straight ahead, seemingly unaware of Gabriel or Raven, her compressed lips expressing the anguish she was feeling. Reece's death, like her husband's, had happened so suddenly, so unexpectedly she wasn't prepared for it. She had come to Old Calico to be looked after, and to give Raven a better life — and now, in a heartbeat, she was once again a single mother trying to raise a rebellious teenage daughter. The big difference, of course, was she no longer had to worry about money. The landslide had made her a rich woman. Years ago Reece had promised her that if anything ever happened to him, everything he owned would go to her. But rich or poor, she thought bitterly, I'm still husbandless, still fending for myself in a world of violence, a man's world, instead of being loved and cared for by someone I love and who loves me.

Distant gunshots interrupted her thinking.

Signaling for Ingrid and Raven to stop, Gabriel spurred his horse almost to the crest of the low hill ahead. There he dismounted and crawled to the top. After a few moments, he remounted and beckoned for them to join him.

They obeyed.

The smell of fire drifted up to them from the canyon in which Old Calico was snuggled. The town had been shaken by the quake and they saw smoke and flames rising from several burning buildings. They could also hear sporadic gunfire.

'Could be looters,' Gabriel warned Ingrid and Raven. 'Stay close to me when we reach town.' They kicked their horses into a trot, descending the long gradual slope that ended at the north end of Old Calico.

'You ever been in an earthquake

before?' Raven asked Gabriel.

'Once. In Colorado. I was about your age an' me'n Pa were in this gold camp tryin' to get the miners to attend our prayer meetin'. Most of 'em refused, and went on drinkin' an' gambling. Pa got sore an' warned 'em that God would seek retribution for their sins. But they only laughed an' rode us out of camp. Right after that the quake hit.' Gabriel grinned, amused by the memory. 'Next time Pa'n me came around, so many miners showed up we had to hold the meetin' outdoors 'cause they couldn't all fit in our tent.'

Shortly, they reached the outskirts of Old Calico. From here they could see the town had been hit harder by the quake than they realized, especially along Main Street where several of the damaged buildings were ablaze.

Looters were everywhere. Mostly riffraff, they were breaking into buildings and stealing whatever they wanted then loading their spoils into a large freight wagon parked outside the Lucky

Nugget Saloon. And when any of the storekeepers tried to interfere, the looters frightened them off by shooting at them.

Despite the looting and chaos, the townspeople were desperately trying to stop the fires from spreading. Volunteer firemen were hosing down the blazing buildings, while the men on the horse-drawn fire-wagon pumped frantically to maintain the water pressure.

Farther along the street, men and women had formed a bucket-line in an effort to douse the flames threatening to destroy the bank and Harley's Feed and Grain store.

The livery stable was only two doors down and Gabriel immediately thought of Brandy. Telling Ingrid to follow him, he spurred the roan along the street and quickly reached the stable. The doors were open and no one seemed to be around.

Dismounting, Gabriel motioned for Ingrid and Raven to keep quiet, drew his Colt and entered the stable. His worst fears were realized: all the stalls were empty. About to leave, he heard a moan. Turning, he saw the hostler's daughter, a slim girl no more than sixteen, sprawled on some hay at the rear.

Yelling for Ingrid to join him, he ran to the girl's side and saw she'd been attacked. Blood streamed from cuts and welts on her face and her dress was ripped down the front.

'It's OK,' Gabriel said softly as she cringed in fear. 'I'm not gonna hurt you.'

Dazed, she whispered something he couldn't understand.

'Who did this?' he asked.

'Men,' she whimpered. 'T-t-tried to stop them from stealing the h-horses, but — ' her voice faltered.

Ingrid and Raven came rushing up. One look at the girl told Ingrid everything. 'Get some water,' she told Raven. 'Hurry! Go!'

Kneeling beside the girl, she stroked her hair and tried to calm her. 'You're going to be fine,' she said soothingly. 'Just fine. Now tell me where your folks are?'

The girl stared at Ingrid, as if trying to place her. 'Pa,' she murmured. 'G-get Pa — '

'Where is he?' said Gabriel.

'F-fires . . . w-went to help p-put out — ' She fainted in his arms.

Just then Raven returned with a bowl of water. Gabriel gently placed the girl in Ingrid's arms and got to his feet.

'You two stay with her while I go help with the fires.'

'Be careful,' Raven begged, clinging to his arm. 'With all them crazy looters running around, you could get shot.'

Looking down at her he saw the fear in her big black eyes and knew she was reliving her father's death. 'Don't worry,' he assured her. 'I'll be careful. Now help your mom.' Gently but firmly he pushed her away and hurried outside.

He stood in the street, immune to the uproar going on around him, looking for the Morgan. Brandy wasn't among the horses tied up outside any of the buildings. Nor was the stallion one of the many panicked, rider-less horses aimlessly running up and down the street.

Determined to find his horse, Gabriel walked toward the center of town. Fires blazed on both sides of him. His eyes began to water and every breath tasted of smoke.

As he approached the undertaker's, he heard gunshots. Suddenly a rider came galloping out of the alley separating the bank from the Lucky Nugget Saloon. Saddle-bags full of money were slung over his shoulder and as he rode, half-turned in the saddle, he fired at someone behind him.

A shot rang out. Hit in the chest, the rider pitched from the saddle, landed, rolled, and laid still. Money spilled from the saddlebags, the loose bills fluttering about the street.

There were looters nearby, most of them still piling stolen goods onto the freight wagon. Gabriel expected them to fight over the money. But strangely, no one went near it.

And moments later, when a man rode out of the alley, a small, slim, handsome man with curly sandy hair and a nickel-plated .44 in his left hand, Gabriel knew why: it was Latigo Rawlins!

'Next one of you saloon-swabbers tries to rob me,' he told the looters, 'dances from a rope!' He let his threat sink in then said: 'Now, pick up my money an' bring it to me in the Nugget. You,' he said to another looter, 'finish loadin' the wagon an' then get ready to move out. There'll be a deputy marshal here soon, maybe even soldiers, an' — '

He broke off, shocked, as he saw Gabriel. Then he slowly grinned and shook his head in a mixture of admiration and disbelief, muttered: 'Harder to lose than a plugged nickel.'

Gabriel, equally shocked to see Latigo alive, said quietly: 'Reckon you know that's my horse you're ridin'.'

'Never figured you'd be back to claim it.'

'Figured wrong.'

'On the prod, huh?'

'Nope. Just lookin' to keep what's mine.'

Latigo, eyes fixed on Gabriel, eased himself out of the saddle in one slow, fluid, graceful movement and stepped to the ground.

'How much you want for him?'

'He ain't for sale.'

'Everything's for sale, *amigo*, includin' a man's soul. Just gotta find the right price.'

Gabriel felt a trickle of sweat run down his back under his shirt. He wasn't afraid of the diminutive gunman, but he did wonder if he could out-draw him.

'Name it,' Latigo continued. He gestured toward the stolen loot piled in the freight wagon. 'I'm a rich man now. Can afford anything I want. Even a stolen horse.'

Gabriel, knowing Latigo was trying

to goad him into drawing, refused to back down. 'Seems to me, that'd be the last thing you'd worry about.'

'Guilty as charged, *amigo*.' Latigo grinned. Deep down he admired Gabriel and hated to have to kill him. 'Ever wonder how it would play out 'tween you'n me?'

'Never,' Gabriel said.

'Never?'

'Never.'

'Me, too,' said Latigo, laughing. He leaned slightly forward, onto the balls of his feet, his left hand dangling just above his gun. 'Any time you're ready, make your play.'

Gabriel, realizing that Latigo, like most deadly gunmen, only wore two guns for show, concentrated on Latigo's left forearm. He knew the lefty's hand might be quicker than his eye, but no matter how fast Latigo was, his forearm had to move first — and Gabriel hoped that that infinitesimal advantage would be enough for him to out-draw the little gunfighter.

Before he could find out he heard Raven call his name.

'Gabe . . . Gaaaabe!'

'Hold it,' he told Latigo. Taking a chance that Latigo would oblige, he turned and saw Raven running toward him.

'What is it?' he asked as she charged up.

'Momma needs you. That girl, the one hurt in the stable, she's bleeding 'tween her legs and Momma's trying to get the doctor to look at her.'

'What's she need me for?'

'There's a bunch of looters stopping her. They're robbin' all the houses on the doctor's street. The folks who live there are trying to hold 'em off and nobody will stop shooting to let Momma pass.'

Gabriel looked questioningly at Latigo.

The little gunman shrugged. 'This'll keep,' he said and handed Gabriel the Morgan's reins. He then winked at Raven. 'Remember me, missy?'

'Sure. You're the man who watered

his horse at our ranch outside Santa Rosa.'

'That's right.' He playfully ruffled her hair. 'Got a good memory.'

'I had a gun trained on you all the time, did you know that?'

'Sure,' he said, playing along. 'Why do you think I high-tailed it out of there.' He grinned at Gabriel, 'I like her grit,' and walked off.

Gabriel stepped into the saddle and pulled Raven up behind him.

'Know what?' she said as they rode off.

'What?'

'I bet he's not that fast.'

'You'd lose that bet.'

'Huh,' she said. 'Well, I still think you could beat him.'

28

Hearing gunfire ahead, Gabriel slowed the Morgan to a walk as he entered Pioneer Avenue, a broad tree-lined street with large wood-frame houses on one side and open country on the other.

He could see Ingrid and the hostler's daughter crouched behind an abandoned buckboard, and farther on down the street a dozen or more looters, hiding behind trees and rocks, shooting at the houses opposite. People in the homes returned their fire, keeping the looters pinned down.

Gabriel reined up as he reached the buckboard, waited for Raven to jump off then dismounted and hunkered down beside Ingrid.

'Thank goodness you're here,' she said, concerned. 'I begged them to stop shooting but the darn fools wouldn't listen to me.' Lowering her voice so only he could hear, she added: 'I've done all I can to slow the bleeding down, but the poor child's already lost a lot of blood — '

Gabriel looked at the young girl slumped against the rear wheel. Her eyes were closed and she looked drained. There was blood on the skirt of her dress and the sight of it, and the looters' lack of compassion, enraged him.

'Which house is the doc's?'

'The middle one,' Ingrid pointed at a green house with white trim around the windows and front door. The glass was broken in the downstairs windows and rifles poked out of two of them. But whoever was shooting wasn't accurate and Gabriel knew it was merely a matter of time before the looters took over.

'Stay here,' he told Ingrid. 'That means you, too,' he warned Raven.

Pulling a Winchester from its scabbard under the saddle, he ducked low and made his way toward the looters.

Trees and rocks and bushes hid him from them, allowing him to work his way around behind them.

He got within spitting distance before one man paused to reload and turned in Gabriel's direction. Alarmed, he dropped his rifle and grabbed for his pistol.

Gabriel shot him. At once the others whirled around. Gabriel shot two more then dived behind some rocks as the looters opened fire.

From behind cover Gabriel angrily pumped round after round into them. And when the rifle was empty he drew his Colt and continued firing.

Unprotected from behind, the looters had no chance. Three more were killed and several others wounded. At the same time, the people in the houses, encouraged by Gabriel's attack, stepped up their shooting.

Caught between a withering cross-fire, the remaining looters threw down their weapons and raised their hands in surrender.

Gabriel emerged from behind the rocks. Keeping the looters covered, he signaled to the people in the houses that the fight was over.

About to signal Ingrid the same message, he saw that she and Raven had already linked hands to form a sling and were carrying the hostler's daughter to the doctor's house. Before they reached there, Dr Guzman and his two teenage sons rushed out and helped them inside.

'Better pray that girl don't die,' Gabriel grimly told the looters. ''Cause if she does, I'll personally see to it you all swing.'

29

By nightfall all the fires were out and any looters who hadn't ridden off with Latigo Rawlins were in jail. Everyone gathered in the partly burned town hall to discuss the restoration of the damaged buildings. That included Gabriel, though it took a lot of persuading by Ingrid and Raven to make him accompany them.

Mayor Adam Pratt, a short, chubby, ebullient man in his sixties, banged his gavel for silence and then showed everyone a telegraph message that he'd received from the newly elected governor of California, Henry Harrison Markham in reply to his request for state assistance and military protection to stop any future looting.

'The Governor assures me that help is on its way,' the mayor said. 'Says there's a trainload of workmen coming to help us dig out any earthquake survivors; and he's dispatching a military detachment from Union Camp some time tomorrow.'

Cheers arose from the townspeople.

'I have more good news, folks. A deputy marshal will be arriving soon from Sacramento to help keep the peace. In the meantime the Governor advised me to appoint a new sheriff as soon as possible.' Pausing, Mayor Pratt searched the faces of the people seated before him, hoping for a response.

None came.

'Come, come, gentlemen,' he encouraged. 'Surely one of you is willing to volunteer your services.'

'Him!' Dr. Guzman pointed at Gabriel. As everyone turned and looked, he added: 'If he hadn't risked his life and stopped those looters from robbing me and my neighbors — perhaps even killing us — Beth Ingram would have surely died.'

'That's for true,' Travis Ingram said. Rising, the burly, balding hostler walked to the back of the room and offered Gabriel his hand. 'Me'n my daughter owe you, mister. And as long as you're living here anythin' I got is yours. So help me God.'

Embarrassed, Gabriel shook hands and accepted the applause from everyone around him.

'How 'bout it, mister?' Mayor Pratt pointed his gavel at Gabriel. 'Can we count on you to uphold the law and protect us?'

Gabriel didn't hesitate. 'Appreciate the offer, Mr Mayor, but — '

Mayor Pratt cut him off. 'Don't have to decide right now, friend. Think on it a while. Discuss it between you' — he beamed at Ingrid and Raven — 'Maybe come morning, you'll feel differently.'

'We'll do that,' Raven said cheekily.

'Rav-ven,' her mother chided.

Everyone laughed.

'Meeting adjourned,' Mayor Pratt said quickly and banged his gavel.

The townspeople started talking among themselves, forming little groups as they slowly began filing out.

Mayor Pratt hurried over to Gabriel, Ingrid and Raven. After offering Ingrid condolences for the loss of her step-brother, he turned to Gabriel, said: 'I don't think I caught your name, sir.'

'Gabe Moonlight,' Gabriel said reluctantly.

'Well, Mr Moonlight, I hope you change your mind and accept the job. Reece Blackwood was a friend of mine. A good friend. And the citizens of Old Calico owe him a lot. Without his enthusiasm and drive to make this a good place to live in, you'd most likely be looking at a ghost town.' He paused, hoping to get a favorable response from Gabriel.

When he didn't, he said: 'Now it may seem odd to you that we'd appoint a stranger as our sheriff. And under normal circumstances, you'd be right. We'd elect him by vote. But I don't need to tell you that these aren't normal circumstances. And since you've proved you're more than capable, and Doc Guzman recommended you, well, that's good enough for me and for everyone else. So I hope you'll reconsider.'

Again he waited for Gabriel to respond and again Gabriel didn't.

The mayor, knowing a stubborn man when he saw one, tipped his hat to Ingrid. 'G'night, ma'am. You too, little lady,' he said to Raven, adding: 'Keep working on him, OK? I got a feeling he's the perfect man for the job.' He hurried off.

'Nice fella,' Gabriel said, meaning it.

Ingrid nodded. 'This is a nice town, too, full of nice people. Be a fine place to settle down.'

Gabriel frowned at her. 'Not suggestin' I take the job, are you?'

'You know me better than that, Gabe.'

'But you wouldn't object if I did?'

'No.'

'How 'bout you?' Gabriel asked Raven. 'Want to throw in your two cents?'

Raven carefully weighed her answer. 'Would I get to be your deputy? When

264

I'm old enough,' she added as he rolled his eyes. 'You'll need someone you can trust and you did say I was responsible — '

'Hush,' her mother said. She lifted her eyes lovingly to Gabriel. 'I guess what we're both saying is, we want you to be a part of our lives. And if that means being sheriff or helping me to run my brother's businesses or even cutting hair at Julius's barbershop — we'll support your decision.'

Gabriel gave a grunt that could have meant anything. ''Case it's slipped your minds, ladies, I'm wanted in three states an' a whole country called Mexico.'

'Who's gonna know that way up here?' Raven said.

'The deputy marshal, for one.'

'I bet he won't,' she said. 'I bet he ain't even heard of you. And even if he has, I bet he won't care. All he'll care about is getting free breakfast, lunch an' dinner and a fast train ride home.'

'Raven, for heaven's sake — '

'It's true, Momma. Dad told me so.

Said whenever ol' Marshal Sheply came to Santa Rosa, or even Las Cruces, that's all he ever talked about — getting stuff for free. Fringe benefits, Dad said he called them. Said he was more worried about that than who needed hanging.'

'I wish you'd stop exaggerating,' Ingrid said. 'Though I must admit,' she added, after a pause, 'Marshal Sheply, God rest his soul, did enjoy the comforts of life.'

'He enjoyed a lot more than that,' Raven said, sounding older than her years. ''Cording to Dad, every cantina floozy in the territory knew him by his first name.'

'All right, that's quite enough, young lady. We don't need any lurid details.'

'I was just trying to prove my point, Momma.'

'Which is?' Gabriel said.

'That lawmen like things easy, same as anyone else.'

'What's that got to do with me bein' wanted?'

'Everything. If you were a deputy marshal where would you want to spin your spurs — Old Calico or some big city like Sacramento or San Francisco?'

Gabriel scowled. 'Spurs don't spin. Rowels spin.'

'Good-God-Almighty.' Raven gave a frustrated snort. 'You're more pernickety than my Dad!'

'Gonna argue, scout, get your facts straight.'

'All right,' she said, undaunted, 'I will. The fact is, Mr Moonlight, sir, you're not wanted for anything in California and that's all the marshal will care about. He'll make sure you're sworn in legally, order the most expensive meal in town an' be on the next train back to Sacramento 'fore he's even wiped the soup stains off his shirt!'

Gabriel chewed on her words for a moment. 'That's what you figure, huh?'

'That's what I know. I may only be fourteen — '

'Thirteen,' corrected her mother. 'You still have three weeks to go before — '

' — but that doesn't mean I'm deaf, dumb or blind,' Raven continued, 'or stupid. While you been moping around the ranch, Momma, and you,' she said to Gabriel, 'been ducking sheriffs, I've been listening and watching and payin' attention to what's going on around me. Been reading, too. By myself in the desert. Books that Dad gave me — '

'So that's where they disappeared to,' Ingrid exclaimed. 'Why didn't you tell me?'

'You wouldn't have believed me. Would've said I was makin' stuff up to get out of helping you do the wash.' She turned back to Gabriel. 'Dad said I gotta be smart if I want to make something of myself. And I do. I want to be rich an' important some day and I'm not gonna let anybody stand in my way!'

'Incredible,' Ingrid said, looking at her daughter as if she didn't know her. 'I swear, Raven, you are the most perplexing child.'

'Why? 'Cause I don't want to grow

up like you, dependent on every man who comes along — '

'Enough! I don't want to hear another word out of you, young lady. And I'm sure Gabriel doesn't either.'

'Fine,' Raven said, disgusted. 'Don't listen to me. See if I care. But one day you'll be sorry. Both of you. So there!'

Floored by her audacity, Gabriel looked at Ingrid for help.

'Don't look at me,' she said wearily. 'I've given up being dumbfounded by her a long time ago.'

Gabriel turned back to Raven. Black eyes full of fight, lips set in a tight, white, stubborn line, jaw thrust out defiantly she made no attempt to avoid his steely gaze.

At that moment he admired her enough to hug her. 'No one's sayin' you're stupid,' he said quietly, 'or it's wrong to have ambitions — '

'Then you will 'least think about it — staying, I mean?'

'Reckon.'

'Not just saying that to shut me up?'

'Nope.'

'Swear?'

'I swear.'

''Cause if you are, and you're gonna ride out on us again, I'd sooner know now so I can get it all cried out of me.'

'Heaven help us,' Ingrid murmured.

Gabriel sighed, hunkered down so his eyes were level with Raven's, and placed his hands fondly on her shoulders.

'Ever known me to lie?'

'No, sir.'

'Go back on my word?'

'No, sir.'

'Reckon that settles it then.' Grasping their hands he led them out of the hall into the cool night air, which still smelled faintly of smoke, and they began walking home.

THE END

We do hope that you have enjoyed reading this large print book.

Did you know that all of our titles are available for purchase?

We publish a wide range of high quality large print books including:
Romances, Mysteries, Classics
General Fiction
Non Fiction and Westerns

Special interest titles available in large print are:
The Little Oxford Dictionary
Music Book, Song Book
Hymn Book, Service Book

Also available from us courtesy of Oxford University Press:
Young Readers' Dictionary
(large print edition)
Young Readers' Thesaurus
(large print edition)

For further information or a free brochure, please contact us at:
Ulverscroft Large Print Books Ltd.,
The Green, Bradgate Road, Anstey,
Leicester, LE7 7FU, England.
Tel: (00 44) 0116 236 4325
Fax: (00 44) 0116 234 0205

A MAN NAMED SHONTO

Ryan Bodie

They were already hanging Marshal Holder when Shonto rode into town. It was one hell of a welcome for a loner with a gun but Shonto sensed that things were going to get even worse. He was right. The marshal's body was still swinging from the cottonwood across the street from his own jailhouse when the town became a bloody battleground. At that point, Shonto had just two choices: shoot to kill or join the lawman in hell.